"We can't keep running forever, Paige. At some point, we'll need to trust the authorities."

"I think it's best if we hold off calling your boss until we have a solid lead to act upon."

"You may be right, although it could be that the information on this SIM card is enough to blow the case wide-open."

"Please, not yet," she begged. "Let's make sure that we don't tip anyone off as to where we are."

Miles didn't say anything for a long moment, but then he nodded. "All right, we'll hold off. For now."

Miles came up to stand beside her as she watched her daughter, and her heart betrayed her by skipping a beat. She didn't want to respond to him, not when she was beyond annoyed with him.

"I'll keep you safe," he murmured softly.

"I know."

He slid his arm around her waist and she leaned against him for a moment, drawing strength from his nearness.

Maybe he was right about calling the authorities. They couldn't stay here indefinitely. Obviously the information on the SIM card was important.

Important enough to kill for.

Laura Scott is a nurse by day and an author by night. She has always loved romance, reading faith-based books by Grace Livingston Hill in her teenage years. She's thrilled to have published sixteen books for Love Inspired Suspense. She has two adult children and lives in Milwaukee, Wisconsin, with her husband of thirty years. Please visit Laura at laurascottbooks.com, as she loves to hear from her readers.

Books by Laura Scott

Love Inspired Suspense

Callahan Confidential

Shielding His Christmas Witness
The Only Witness

SWAT: Top Cops

Wrongly Accused
Down to the Wire
Under the Lawman's Protection
Forgotten Memories
Holiday on the Run
Mirror Image

Visit the Author Profile page at Harlequin.com for more titles.

THE ONLY WITNESS

LAURA SCOTT

HARLEQUIN® LOVE INSPIRED® SUSPENSE

Recycling programs for this product may not exist in your area.

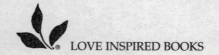

LOVE INSPIRED BOOKS

ISBN-13: 978-0-373-67803-7

The Only Witness

Copyright © 2017 by Laura Iding

www.Harlequin.com

Printed in U.S.A.

Whoever dwells in the shelter of the Most High
will rest in the shadow of the Almighty.
–Psalms 91:1

This book is dedicated to my cousin Carie Binger.
Thanks for all the great childhood memories, skiing
and boating on the Wisconsin River. Love you!

ONE

A loud crash from her five-year-old daughter's room startled Paige Olson, causing her to drop the lasagna pan she'd been washing.

"Abby?" Grabbing the dishtowel on the counter, Paige quickly dried her hands, then tossed it aside to hurry over to the short hallway of her cozy two-bedroom house. Off the hallway was a bathroom, with her daughter's room on one side and hers on the other. "Sweetie, are you all right?"

Stepping into her daughter's bedroom, her gaze instantly found the source of the crash. Abby's tablet was lying face down on the scuffed hardwood floor.

Paige had told her ex-husband that the tablet was too expensive for a five-year-old, but he hadn't listened. Not that Travis ever cared about her opinions.

"Abby, where are you?" Paige noticed that Ellie, her little girl's favorite stuffed elephant, wasn't anywhere in sight, and quickly deduced that her daughter likely had the toy clutched in her arms under the bed. Abby often crawled beneath her bed during thunderstorms, too. Paige had just dropped to her knees to check when a loud crash, followed by a sharp report, rang through the house.

"What in the world?" Paige lifted her head over the edge of Abby's bed, shocked to see that her daughter's bedroom window was broken.

A second bang echoed sharply and it took Paige a moment to figure out that the noise was gunfire.

Someone was shooting at her house!

Heart thundering in her chest, she crouched beside the bed, trying to think. Her phone was in the kitchen, but she couldn't leave Abby alone. She dropped down to all fours, peering beneath the bed frame. "Abby?" She kept her voice low. "We need to get out of here."

Her daughter stared at her from under the bed with wide tear-stained eyes and shook her head.

Paige tried to smile reassuringly. "Come on, sweetie, someone broke your window. We need to go someplace safe."

Abby stared at her for a moment longer, then crawled slowly across the floor, dragging Ellie the pink elephant along with her. Paige thought it was strange that Abby didn't say anything, but right now she had bigger worries.

She had no idea why on earth anyone would

shoot at her house. There must be some sort of crime in progress nearby and the gunfire had gone wide, hitting her house instead of the intended target. Nothing else made sense, and Paige desperately needed her phone to call for help.

When Abby was close enough, she reached for the little girl, gently pulling her into a warm hug. Abby buried her face in her mother's shoulder, her entire body shaking with fear.

"Shh, it's okay. We're going to be fine, you'll see." Paige stayed on her hands and knees, awkwardly holding Abby up against her with one hand as she maneuvered across the hardwood floor toward the hallway.

As she reached the opening, she froze, wondering for the first time if she was heading into a trap. What if the gunfire was aimed at her house on purpose? What if there were bad guys making their way inside through the front door, waiting for her and Abby to head in that direction?

They had nothing worth stealing, but robbers wouldn't know that. Violent crime in the city had recently been on the rise.

The bathroom was right next to Abby's room, so she scuttled in that direction, practically diving inside. She quickly shut the door, locking it behind her. A frantic glance around the tiny space didn't reveal much that could be used as a barrier against the door to prevent anyone from getting inside.

Rising to her feet, she rifled through the medicine cabinet, finding a can of hairspray that might be used as a weapon. Then she lifted Abby up and into the tub, pulling the shower curtain closed. She stretched out, so they were lying on the bottom of the ceramic tub, her body protectively covering her daughter's.

Anyone trying to hurt them would have to get through her first.

Surely the neighbors would call the police. Mrs. Stevenson, known for being the area gossip, was probably alerting the authorities right now.

Paige snuggled Abby close, pressing a kiss to her forehead. "We're safe now. I won't leave you alone."

Abby didn't answer, and the silent tears coursing down her face ripped a hole in Paige's heart.

Dear Lord, please don't let anything happen to us!

Homicide Detective Miles Callahan pulled up in front of Paige Olson's small rectangular house and shut off the engine. The hour wasn't too late, just past seven thirty in the evening, but darkness had fallen, and there was a definite chill in the late-March air. Lights blazed from her windows, indicating Paige was home. Good. The sooner he could talk to her, the better.

He rubbed his burning eyes, knowing he couldn't sleep until he discovered who'd killed his college roommate, Jason Whitfield. Jason worked at Sci-Tech, Inc., and had confided in Miles about the trouble he was having with his boss, Travis Olson. Unfortunately, Jason had been killed before he could give Miles the specifics. After spending hours searching for Travis, Miles had decided to visit the guy's ex-wife to see if she knew where he was. If she did, he intended to keep pushing forward, working the case. If she didn't, he might have to grab a few hours of shut-eye, since he'd been up since three o'clock in the morning.

Miles slid out from behind the wheel, closing the car door behind him. He'd only taken one step toward the small ranch home when the sound of gunfire burst through the night.

Instinctively, Miles pulled his weapon from his shoulder holster and dropped into a crouch behind his car, scanning the area around him. He didn't see any sign of anyone lurking around, but that didn't mean much. The first shot was quickly followed by another, and he estimated that the gunman must be stationed somewhere behind the house.

He quickly called for backup, but then couldn't

just sit there, waiting. Not when he knew that Travis Olson's ex-wife and their young daughter were likely somewhere inside.

What if one of them had been hit? What if Travis Olson was inside, too, or he'd gone off the deep end, killing Jason and now attempting to eliminate everyone close to him? Jason had given Miles the impression that Travis was a man on the edge.

Miles kept his head down as he ran toward the front door. Plastering himself against the side of the gray-and-white structure, he held his gun pointing upward as he listened intently.

Silence.

All of his senses on alert, he tried the front door. The screen door wasn't locked, but the inside door was. It was also solid and sturdy, so he quickly edged over to the large picture window. Miles kicked the window with his boot, shattering the glass. He was wearing a black leather jacket and used his elbow to brush away the broken shards that remained before throwing his leg over the sill and climbing inside.

"Mrs. Olson?" he called loudly, looking around. The living room was open to the kitchen, and there was no one in the immediate area. He could see splashes of water on the counter near a dishtowel. To the left of the living room/kitchen area was a short hallway leading to what he assumed were the bedrooms.

He could make out the glow of the light from the bedroom closest to the rear of the house. Miles kept his back to the wall as he edged closer.

"Mrs. Olson? This is Detective Callahan from the Milwaukee Police Department. I heard gunfire. Are you or your daughter hurt?"

Still nothing, and a sick feeling coiled low in his belly. What if he was too late? He made his way down the hall toward the bedroom, bracing himself for the worst.

Frilly pink curtains ruffled in the breeze coming in through a broken window. A tablet was lying upside down on the floor surrounded by bits of glass, but thankfully no blood and no injured people.

He took a moment to check under the bed and look in the closet before turning back the way he'd come. The hallway stretched toward the front of the house, and he could see there were two additional doors; the one farthest away was open, could be another bedroom, while the door in the middle was closed.

The bathroom?

He tested the door handle and found it locked. "Mrs. Olson, I'm a Milwaukee police detective and I have backup officers on the way. Are either of you hurt? There will be an ambulance, too, if needed."

"We're not hurt." The woman's voice sounded muffled and he couldn't deny the feeling of relief.

"I'm glad. Why don't you let me in? I'll keep you safe from harm."

"How do you know who I am?" Suspicion laced her tone and Miles had to give the woman credit. She might be scared to death, but she was thinking things through in a logical manner.

She had no reason to trust him.

"I came here to ask for help in locating your ex-husband." Miles wanted to reassure her that he wasn't there to hurt her.

"Why do you want to find Travis?"

"I'm working on a case and need to ask him a few questions, that's all."

Another gunshot boomed loudly and he dropped to his knees, a surge of adrenaline sending his heart thumping as he searched frantically for the source of the gunshot.

A scream echoed from inside the bathroom. Without hesitation, he slammed into the flimsy door with his shoulder, bursting inside. The bathroom window had a bullet hole and the shower curtain was closed over the tub.

He pushed the curtain aside, and found a slim woman he guessed to be in her late twenties, with glossy brown hair and green-gold eyes behind oval eyeglasses. She was clutching a small girl who looked just like her, sans glasses. "Why are they shooting at us?" Paige Olson asked hoarsely.

"I don't know, but we need to get out of here." Miles took her arm and helped her out of the tub, urging her out of the small bathroom to the kitchen and living room area.

"I don't understand." Her voice bordered on panic, not that he could blame her. "What's going on?"

He had no idea what was happening, other than the strong possibility that the shooter outside might be related to Jason's death.

"This way," he said in a low voice, gesturing to the far side of the living room. There was a side window facing in the opposite direction from where he estimated the shooter was located. And it wasn't far from where he'd left his car. They needed to get away from here as soon as possible.

He raised the window sash and pulled the screen out of the way.

"Maybe we should go into the basement," Paige whispered.

"It's better if we're not trapped." He wasn't about to wait around a moment longer than necessary. When he had the window clear, he shrugged off his black leather jacket and held it out to her. "Put this on."

She didn't let go of her daughter, but managed

to get her arms into the sleeves. When she was ready, he went outside first, then held out his hands. "It might be easier for me to hold your daughter."

The child, who hadn't spoken a word, shrank closer to her mother, clinging like a little monkey. He stepped back and held out a hand. "Never mind. Here, lean on me."

Paige threw one leg over the sill, then ducked beneath the frame. She teetered there for a moment, so he quickly caught her in his arms and hauled her the rest of the way out of the window.

"See my car there along the curb?" He gestured to his navy blue sedan.

"Yes."

"We're getting out of here before anything else happens."

She gave a terse nod, trusting him to keep them safe. He shielded them as best he could as they moved quickly across the snow-patched frozen ground to his car.

He didn't have a booster seat for the child, but that wasn't his top priority. Paige slid into the backseat with her daughter, leaving him to get behind the wheel. He quickly started the engine and put the car in gear.

Crack! Another gunshot echoed through the night, hitting the passenger side of his vehicle with a loud thud.

"Are you okay? You're not hurt?"

"We're okay," Paige said in a muffled tone.

The faint sound of police sirens reached his ears, but Miles didn't hesitate. He stomped hard on the accelerator and pulled away from the curb, speeding down the street as fast as possible, putting badly needed distance between his car and the gunman.

Leaving the scene of a crime was against the rules, but at the moment he was more concerned with making sure that Paige Olson and her daughter were safe.

They were clearly in danger, but why? Who would shoot at a woman and a child? Deep in his gut, he sensed there had to be a link between the shooter who'd just hit Paige's house and his buddy's murder.

He needed to figure it out, before any more blood was shed.

Thirty minutes after they'd left her normally quiet and safe neighborhood behind, Paige still couldn't relax. The sound of gunfire continued to echo in her mind, over and over again until she thought she might scream.

She knew she should be glad that the police detective had risked his life to save them, but she couldn't ignore the fact that he'd only come to see her in the first place because of Travis.

For a moment she squeezed her eyes shut in frustrated anger. Her ex-husband had cheated on her practically from the moment they'd gotten married, although she hadn't found out about the other women he went out with until Abby was born and one of the women showed up at the hospital looking for Travis.

He'd apologized to Paige and promised to be faithful, but of course that hadn't lasted more than a couple of months. She finally divorced him when Abby was two and she'd made it a point to do her best to get along with him, for their daughter's sake.

But now it looked as if Travis was in trouble again. He'd called her a few weeks ago, asking if she'd keep Abby over the weekend he was supposed to take her. Of course she'd agreed, but she'd also sensed tension in his tone.

She'd asked what was wrong and he blamed his stress on work. As he was the director of research and development for Sci-Tech, she hadn't thought too much about it.

But now she couldn't help but wonder if there had been more to it than that.

Paige took several deep breaths, burying her face in the collar of the detective's black leather jacket. The scent of leather, combined with his aftershave, was surprisingly calming. She turned her attention to her daughter. Abby was plastered against her, hanging on as if she'd never let go. She was glad to realize that Abby had managed to keep a firm grip on Ellie. Having her favorite toy with her should assist in keeping her calm.

"Hey, Abby, you can sit up if you like. We're safe now. The nice policeman, Detective…" She frowned, forgetting the guy's name.

"Miles," he supplied in a low, masculine tone.

"Detective Miles helped us get away."

Abby moved her head a bit, as if seeking a more comfortable angle, but didn't say anything in response.

"Mrs. Olson?" He glanced at her in the rear-view mirror.

"You may as well call me Paige." She forced a smile. The detective was wearing a long-sleeved light blue shirt and dark slacks, and she wondered if he was cold, since she still had his jacket. "Thanks for helping us."

"You're welcome. Please, call me Miles." He cleared his throat. "Will you walk me through the events that happened before I arrived?"

She swallowed hard. "I was finishing up the dinner dishes while Abby was playing in her room. I heard a crash and hurried over to see she'd dropped her tablet. She must have been afraid that I'd yell at her, because she was hiding under the bed."

"Go on," he urged.

"When I bent down to check if she was under there, the window shattered. I heard a loud bang and realized that someone was shooting at the house. I was able to get Abby to come out and my plan was to hide in the bathroom until the police arrived."

"Did you call them?"

"No." She realized her phone was still on the kitchen counter. "I didn't have my phone. I thought about going back to the kitchen, but then I wondered if it might be better to hide." She didn't want to say exactly what she'd thought, since she knew Abby was listening.

"I was outside the front of your house when I heard the gunshots," he said.

Now that it was over, she was grateful for his impeccable timing. "I'm glad."

"When was the last time you spoke to your ex-husband?" Miles asked.

She grimaced. "Last week. He was supposed to take Abby for the weekend, but he called to cancel again."

"Again?"

"He's supposed to take her every other weekend, but he's canceled three times in a row. But I know he keeps in touch with Abby on ChatTime, right, Abby?"

Her daughter pressed her face more firmly against Paige's neck but nodded her head.

"ChatTime?" Miles repeated. "They communicate face-to-face using the tablet?"

"Yes. It was Travis's idea, even though I've tried to tell him that ChatTime isn't the same as spending time together actually doing things." Yet another bone of contention between them.

"Abby? Did you talk to your daddy tonight?" Miles asked.

Paige was surprised when every muscle in her daughter's body went tense.

"Abby, honey, it's okay," she murmured, stroking the child's hair, the exact same color as her own. "We're safe now. I'm not mad at you for dropping the tablet. We can always get another one."

Abby didn't relax or lift her head, or indicate in any way that she'd heard either of them talking, even though Paige was certain she had.

"Abby, please say something." Her motherly instincts were screaming at her that something was wrong with her daughter. But what?

"Are you sure she's not hurt?" Miles asked in a concerned tone.

"I don't know." Paige ran her hands up and down Abby's small body, feeling for anything abnormal.

When her daughter shook her head from side to side, she stopped. "Are you hurt?" she asked.

Another head shake.

"Are you upset about something?"

Definite head nod up and down.

"What's wrong? Will you tell me why you're upset?"

Another head shake no.

"Why won't you talk to me?" Paige asked helplessly.

"She's probably still scared from everything that's happened," Miles said, as if trying to reassure her. "Rather than taking you to the police station, we'll stay at a motel for the rest of the night. Tomorrow you'll need to give a statement. Maybe Abby will feel better by then, too."

"Did you hear that, Abby? Detective Miles is taking us to a motel. Maybe they'll have a swimming pool. Wouldn't that be fun?"

No response.

Fear squeezed like a fist around her heart. Abby loved to swim. She was normally a bright, talkative little girl. In fact, her kindergarten teacher sent notes home on a weekly basis complaining about Abby being such a chatterbox.

Paige thought back to when she'd heard the tablet drop on the floor, the way her daughter had been hiding under the bed, clutching her stuffed elephant with teary eyes, moments before Paige heard the sound of gunfire.

And she knew something was terribly wrong.

More than just the gunfire they'd experienced had caused such a drastic change in her daughter. But what?

TWO

Miles kept an eye on the road behind him, making sure there wasn't anyone following them as he drove through the night. The hour wasn't that late, so there was more traffic than he would have liked, forcing him to make several turns, heading in a zigzag pattern to the Ravenswood Motel, a place he'd learned about a few months ago when his older brother, Marc, had hidden out there with a witness. A witness that he'd ended up marrying just a month ago.

As happy as he was for Marc, no way was he going down that same path. Serious relationships were not for him.

Pulling his thoughts back to the situation at hand, Miles tried to put the puzzle pieces of his case together. Jason's body had been found in a Dumpster a few minutes before three o'clock in the morning, after succumbing to injuries from a gunshot wound to the chest. The only person Jason had seemed to have issues with was his boss, Travis Olson. Miles had gone to Sci-Tech first, but had been told that Travis wasn't there. He'd gone to Olson's condo, but he hadn't been there, either. So he'd dug into Travis Olson's background, finding out about his ex-wife, Paige, and their daughter, Abigail. So he'd headed over, only to find Travis's ex caught in the middle of an ambush.

Coincidence? Not likely, although it would be nice to have ballistics prove a connection. Maybe the slugs they'd find in Paige's house would match the type that had been used on Jason.

But why shoot at the woman and child in the first place? That was another link he couldn't ignore.

He wasn't going to allow anything to happen to an innocent woman and her child, so if that meant bypassing normal police procedures, then fine. Their safety had to come first.

"Miles?" Paige's voice was soft, tentative.

"Yes?" He met her gaze in the rearview mirror.

"When do you think I'll be able to take Abby home?"

He grimaced and shook his head. "Not anytime soon, unfortunately. Once the crime scene techs have finished gathering evidence, you can authorize the repairs to the windows, but that's it. You can't return until we know who's after you and why."

"Don't you think it might be a mistake? That maybe some other house was the real target?" There was a thin thread of hope in her voice, one that he didn't like having to destroy with the blunt truth.

"No, I don't." He wished there was something to say to make her feel better. "How much do you know about your husband's work at Sci-Tech?"

"Ex-husband," she corrected tersely. "Not a lot. I know he's involved in artificial intelligence, but he didn't confide in me about the specifics. In fact, he always made a point to remind me that his work is highly confidential."

Highly confidential? That's exactly what Jason Whitfield had told him when he'd asked about what he was working on. Was it possible Sci-Tech was doing classified work for the government?

"How long have you been divorced?"

"Three years." He caught a glimpse of her pale hand as she smoothed her palm over her daughter's back.

"A lot can change in three years. Do you think his work is still considered highly confidential?"

She nodded, her lips pressing together in a thin line. "The last time we spoke, he said things were stressful at work because they were trying to solve a technical glitch in some sort of software that could revolutionize the artificial intelligence used to create artificial limbs and other medically necessary devices."

Interesting. So, what had gone wrong? Why had Jason been murdered? His friend had mentioned stress at work, too, but Miles thought he was speaking about his issues with his boss, not the actual work itself. Miles needed more information on Sci-Tech, but so far all his efforts to glean more had been in vain. He'd spent hours calling around the company, asking to speak to various team leaders, only to be completely stonewalled.

So far, Travis Olson and Sci-Tech were the only two links between Jason's murder and the gunshots at Paige's house.

"Why do you keep asking about my ex-husband?"

He swallowed hard, trying to think of how much to tell her. "Have you heard the name Jason Whitfield?"

Paige frowned. "It sounds familiar, but I can't be sure."

He wasn't surprised. Since she'd been divorced from Travis for three years, he doubted they spoke about things related to his job anymore. "He worked for your ex-husband at Sci-Tech."

"Worked?" She'd picked up on his use of past tense. "Did he quit?"

"Jason was found shot to death early this

morning. I'm a homicide detective investigating his murder."

She sucked in a harsh breath. "And you think the same gunman came to my house looking for Travis?"

He didn't answer right away, because she had a point. Just because Travis and Jason hadn't gotten along didn't mean that Olson killed his buddy. Paige could have nailed the truth that someone else was after both Jason and Travis. Either way, something strange was obviously going on.

"I'm not sure," he answered truthfully. "I was hoping your ex-husband would be able to give me more information. How's Abby?" he asked, changing the subject. He turned right and caught a glimpse of the sign for the Ravenswood Motel.

"Sleeping." Her brow furrowed. "I'm worried about her, though."

He didn't know anything about kids, had avoided serious entanglements after watching his girlfriend, Dawn Ebbe, die of leukemia right after college. She'd suffered for a long time, dying far too young. His heart had ached for her, wishing there was more he could do to help, but she'd slipped away in her sleep, leaving him feeling sad, frustrated, angry and alone.

From that moment on, he'd decided to live his life to the fullest, the way Dawn had tried to do before she became so sick and weak she couldn't move around on her own. His goal was to enjoy life, without getting seriously involved.

His phone rang, and he used the hands-free function to answer it. "Callahan."

"Miles? This is Detective Lisa Krantz."

He tried to place her in his memory. Oh, yeah, he remembered now, she was a tall blonde, with a brand-new gold shield. "Detective, what's up?"

"There's been a break-in at your house. The place has been tossed, as if someone was looking for something."

"When?"

"One of the neighbors called it in about fifteen minutes ago, and there happened to be a uniform in the area. I stopped by to take a look, but I have another call so I'm heading across town now. I figured you'd want to know."

"I do, thanks. I'll head over there now to see for myself." He disconnected, his thoughts whirling.

Was this break-in related to Jason's murder? Had the killer discovered they were friends? That Jason had called Miles several times in the past few weeks?

Or was the break-in related to something else entirely?

Paige frowned when Miles executed a sharp U-turn, heading back the way they'd come. "Do you think it's smart to go there? What if there's a gunman waiting for you, too?"

"There are officers on the scene, and I'll protect you. Besides, we won't stay long."

She didn't like being dependent on Miles, but what other choice did she have? Being left at a motel room with Abby and no vehicle to get away if needed didn't sound like a good option, either.

It didn't take Miles long to pull into the driveway of a small red-brick house with black shutters and white trim. Abby curled against her, still clinging to her neck as if she'd never let go.

"Sit tight. I'll be right back." Miles pushed open the driver's door as a short, stocky uniformed officer came out to meet him.

The car seemed empty without his reassuring presence. She listened as the two of them spoke.

"Fair amount of damage," the cop said. "Everything's a mess. It's obvious they were looking for something."

"Check for fingerprints, maybe we'll get a hit," Miles told him. "I want to take a look. Will you stay out here and keep an eye on my passengers?"

The uniformed officer nodded. "Sure. No problem."

"Hey, Abby," Paige said in an effort to reassure her daughter. "There's another policeman here, do you see him?" She wanted the little girl to know they were safe, but Abby didn't lift her head to look around.

The sick feeling crept over her again, warning her that something was seriously wrong. Paige continued talking to Abby in soft, gentle tones, telling her that the policemen would put the bad men with guns away and keep them safe.

When that didn't work, she offered a quick prayer.

"Dear Lord, please keep us safe and help Abby feel better, Amen."

Normally her daughter would join in to say *Amen*, but not this time. Paige knew she couldn't push, that Abby would speak when she was ready.

But the continued silence bothered her. A lot.

Miles returned a few minutes later, his expression grim. He carried a small duffel bag that he tossed into the trunk.

"Call me if you get a hit from any fingerprints," he said to the officer.

"Will do."

He slid behind the wheel and backed out of the driveway. He didn't speak until they were back on the highway headed to the motel.

"Do you think the officer is right? That someone was looking for something inside your home?"

"Yeah, that's the only thing that makes sense," he said in a clipped tone.

"Something related to your case?"

"That's exactly what I need to figure out." He used his hands-free function to make another phone call. "Captain?" he said when a gruff voice answered. "This is Callahan."

"I can't believe you left the scene of the crime!" Captain O'Dell's tone was hoarse, as if he'd been yelling all day long and was losing his voice.

"I need 24/7 protection for Paige Olson and her daughter. Will you free up a couple of uniforms?"

"With our budget cuts? No way. We're already short-handed as it is. Find a safe place to stash her, then report in, understand?"

"Yeah. Got it."

Paige swallowed hard and tried not to let her fear show. "Thanks for trying. I'm sure we'll be fine at the motel. I'd just—feel better if I had a car, or a way to get to safety in case something happens." She didn't love Travis anymore, but he was still her daughter's father and she was worried about him, as well.

Miles let out a heavy sigh. "Don't worry, I'm not leaving you at the motel alone."

He wasn't? "But your boss, your captain said…"

"I know what he said, but I'm not abandoning you. I'll check in with him tomorrow."

The wave of relief caught her off guard. Since

when did she trust a man? Never in the years since her divorce.

Logically, she knew this was different. Miles wasn't interested in her on a personal level. He was just being kind. And protective.

She told herself she was glad there was only a professional courtesy between them. Sure, he was handsome with his dark brown hair, chiseled features and big, muscular physique. And yes, maybe he smelled good, too. But after spending the last three years piecing her life back together, taking on an accounting job at a firm that allowed her to work at home so she could remain independent yet support her daughter, she finally felt as if she had her life back on track.

No way was she willing to risk changing anything now.

"Number twelve is our room." Miles wasn't happy that there hadn't been connecting rooms available, but at least this one had two double beds.

Paige pursed her lips, but didn't argue. "Okay."

He parked the car in front of their Ravenswood Motel room and shut off the engine. "Do you need help with Abby?"

"No, I have her." He came around to open her passenger-side door, grimacing at the bullet hole he found in the back fender. Any closer and the gunman might have taken out a tire, making escape impossible.

She took his outstretched hand, and a jolt of awareness tingled up his arm. He scowled, not liking his inadvertent response to her. Paige was the type of woman who had serious relationship written all over her.

Besides, he was responsible for her safety.

"Thanks," she whispered, releasing his hand once she was out of the car and steady on her feet. Abby was still draped over her mother, but her limbs were lax as she slept.

He was glad the child was able to get some rest, and hoped she'd feel better in the morning.

After unlocking the door, he held it open so Paige could go through first. He turned on one lamp, casting a warm glow over the interior of the room.

Choosing the bed closest to the bathroom, Paige bent down and awkwardly pulled the polyester bedspread and blanket out of the way with one hand, so she could set Abby down on the mattress. The child squirmed a bit, before relaxing against the pillows.

Paige stared down at her daughter for a long moment before turning toward him. "I'll share this bed with Abby, I want to be close by in case she has nightmares."

"Understood." Exhaustion weighed him down,

but he shoved it away, trying to focus on what still needed to be done. After setting one of the room key cards on the table between the double beds, he tucked the other one into his pocket. "I'm going outside for a couple minutes to make a quick call. You'll be okay?"

Paige nodded, then slipped out of his jacket. "Here you can have this back."

He wanted to tell her to keep it, but since he had no idea how long he'd be outside, he decided he might need it to stay warm. However, it wasn't easy to ignore her lemony scent clinging to the fabric as he drew on the jacket.

When he turned toward the door, she called out to him. "Miles?"

He glanced over his shoulder. "Yeah?"

"I accidentally left Abby's stuffed elephant in the backseat. Will you bring it in with you?"

He hadn't even noticed the child clutching a toy, but for some reason, the idea that she had something from her home to comfort her made him smile. "Sure, no problem."

"Thanks." The expression on her lovely face was strained, as if she was hanging on by a thread. Understandable, since it wasn't every day that a woman was forced to flee from a gunman with her young daughter in tow.

The air outside seemed colder after the warm interior of the motel room. Hunching his shoulders against the brisk wind, he opened the back door and found the pink elephant. He took it around to the front seat so he wouldn't forget to take it back inside with him.

Miles dialed his brother Mitch, who thankfully answered on the second ring. "Miles? What's up?"

"Someone trashed my place." Remembering the mess ticked him off all over again. "Do you have time to head over there, make sure things are locked up once they're finished processing the evidence?"

Mitch whistled beneath his breath. "Is the break-in related to something you're currently working on?"

"Maybe." Either his current case, or a cold one. Miles didn't want to mention the fact that he'd also been working on his father's murder investigation in his spare time. Nine months ago, Max Callahan had been the Milwaukee chief of police. He'd gone out to the scene of an officer-involved shooting as a sign of support for his colleagues, when someone had gunned him down. The entire Callahan clan still mourned his passing, and Miles wanted nothing more than to find the perpetrator who'd killed their father.

He'd discovered that the bullet responsible for his father's death had been retained in the evidence room, but now it was missing, which made him suspicious about what was going on related to his dad's case.

But right now, he had more urgent issues to worry about. "I'd join you, but I need to keep watch over a victim and her daughter."

"Yeah, okay. Anything else?"

Miles was grateful that he had his family to fall back on. He was the second oldest, behind Marc. Mitch was born two years after him. Michael was fourth in line and the twins, Matthew and Madison, Maddy for short, were the youngest.

"Nothing right now, but I'll be in touch."

"Keep your head down, bro, you hear?"

Miles placed a second call to the dispatch center, asking for the officers who'd been sent to the Olson residence. He was given the name and number of Bernie Nowak. Nowak picked up after several rings and sounded grumpy about it.

"What? I'm busy."

"Hey, Bernie, this is Miles Callahan. What did you find so far?"

"Where are you?" Bernie demanded. He'd been on the force for twenty-four years and was literally counting the days till he could retire. "You weren't supposed to leave the scene."

"The shooter kept coming, even managed to nick my car with a bullet, so I decided saving lives was more important than waiting for you guys."

Bernie grunted. "Yeah, well, we found two

slugs, both from a twenty-two-caliber rifle. Not the weapon of choice for your average punk crook."

Maybe not, but it was the same caliber bullet found at the scene of Jason's murder. "Anything else?"

"Got several broken windows and a busted-up tablet in the kid's room, but that's about it. We won't know if anything is missing until the owner comes in and does a walk-through."

"I'll pass that along, thanks." Miles disconnected and stared thoughtfully out the window.

Robbery was not the motive here. The reason the shooter used a twenty-two rifle was so they could stay several yards back, shooting at Paige from a distance. Easier to kill people that way, than getting up close and personal with a handgun.

More accurate, too.

The twenty-two caliber bullet was one link between the two crimes, not counting the break-in at his place. But he still had more questions than answers. What did it all mean? Miles was glad he had his laptop with him, or the guys who'd tossed his house would have taken it. At least he could still work Jason's case.

With a flick of his wrist, he started the car and drove away from their room, choosing to park around the corner of the building. With the stuffed elephant under his arm, he slid out from behind the wheel, then grabbed the computer case and his duffel out of the trunk.

After entering the motel room as quietly as possible, he wasn't surprised to find that Paige was still awake, watching the doorway with wide eyes. She was stretched out beside her daughter, but didn't look at all relaxed, her expression troubled.

"Are you all right?" he asked, closing the door softly behind him.

"I don't think I'll be able to sleep."

"I know it's not easy, but you need to try and get some rest." He was a fine one to talk, since he'd been up for eighteen hours straight. He set the computer and duffel bag down, then took the stuffed elephant over to her. "Here."

"Thanks." Paige tucked the elephant next to Abby, keeping the toy close at hand for when she woke up.

The little girl's brow was furrowed, as if she was remembering bad things even in sleep. He stood for a moment, wishing there was something he could do to ease the child's burden. It wasn't right that an innocent little girl had to be caught in the middle of this mess.

"Every time I close my eyes, I hear gunshots."

He slid his hands into his pockets, to prevent himself from offering comfort. "Try to think of something nice and soothing, like lying in a hammock or listening to the ocean."

"Good advice. I'll try praying."

Miles lifted a brow, but didn't comment. He and his siblings had been raised to have faith in God, but watching Dawn get sicker and sicker until she was nothing more than skin and bones had put a severe dent in his faith. Their church pastor had said it was part of God's plan, but he didn't understand that at all. Dawn was barely twenty-five years old, what was so important in God's plan that she had to die? To never fall in love, get married, have children...

He abruptly pulled himself back from that train of thought and took a step back. Watching Paige interact with her daughter was bringing back memories better left buried. "Good idea."

Miles stripped off his jacket and washed up in the bathroom. When he emerged, Paige's eyes were closed, although he sensed she wasn't asleep.

He left the light on in the bathroom for the child's sake, but closed the door so it wouldn't disturb them. Crossing over to the desk, he booted up the computer.

The sooner he found Travis Olson, the better. The man was either part of the reason Jason had died, or he was a target, as well.

So far Miles hadn't found much to go on, but he was determined to keep trying. He wished he'd asked Jason more about what was bothering him at work, but then again, he hadn't counted on his friend being murdered.

Miles had barely started his search when he heard the covers rustling on the bed.

Abby? Or Paige? He turned in his seat and saw that Abby was sitting bolt upright, staring at him as if he were some sort of monster.

Then she let out a shrill scream.

THREE

"Abby, I'm right here. Mommy is right here." Paige cradled her daughter in her arms, trying to cut through the haze of Abby's nightmare. "It's okay, we're safe. Shh…everything is okay."

"Am I scaring her?" Miles asked softly. He shut the laptop and turned on the lamp so that Abby could see him more clearly.

Paige wasn't sure what had set her daughter off, but Abby's screaming abruptly stopped and she turned, burrowing her face against Paige's chest, tears soaking through her shirt.

"It's okay," Paige repeated, feeling helpless as she stroked her hand down the child's back. "We're safe here. Miles will protect us from harm."

"Maybe the glow of the computer made me look scary," Miles offered in an apologetic tone.

"It was more likely a nightmare," Paige whispered with a wan smile.

Abby abruptly shook her head, causing Paige to frown and look down at her.

"No? It wasn't a nightmare?" she asked.

Head shake. No.

"Did you think Miles was a bad guy?" Paige asked, trying to understand what was going on in her daughter's tortured mind.

Another head shake.

"What frightened you?" Paige looked around the room in confusion. It was your average motel room, nothing unique or strange about it.

"Was it the computer?" Miles asked. "Did the computer screen frighten you, Abby?"

Head nod.

Paige blinked, and lifted her gaze to meet his. "How did you know?"

"The tablet."

Before Paige could say anything, Abby nodded again, then turned her head so that she could see Miles. Paige had the impression her daughter wanted Miles to figure out what was bothering her, that she was looking to him for help. But why wouldn't Abby just tell them?

"You saw something scary on the tablet, didn't you, Abby?" Miles's voice was gentle. "That's why you dropped it."

Head nod, up and down.

"Oh, no," Paige whispered. "Was it your daddy?"

Abby nodded, her face scrunching up as if she didn't want to remember.

Paige's stomach clenched with fear. "Why won't you talk to me, Abby? Will you please tell us what you saw?"

Her daughter shook her head as two fat tears rolled down her cheeks.

"It's all right, Abby," Miles said in a soft, reassuring voice. "You've been a big help already. Don't be scared. I'll keep you and your mom safe."

Paige swallowed past the hard lump in her throat, trying to imagine what her daughter might have seen. Obviously something through the ChatTime link that she'd had with her father, but what?

Or *who*?

A shiver ran down Paige's spine, an icy coldness pooling in the small of her back. Was it possible Abby had seen something she shouldn't have? Was that the reason gunmen had come to the house?

No, the timing between Abby dropping the tablet and the gunfire seemed too close for that.

"Paige? Are you sure you don't have any idea where your ex-husband is? It's really important that I find him."

"The only places I know that he goes to are either work or his condo." She lifted one shoulder, feeling helpless. "Did you check?"

"I couldn't get past the front desk at Sci-Tech, but I did go to his condo. He didn't answer the door and the neighbors claimed they hadn't seen him in the past day or so." Miles glanced at her hopefully. "Do you have a key to his place?"

She grimaced. Having a key meant risking walking in on Travis with one of his lady friends. No, thank you. "Never wanted one."

"I'll see if we can't get a search warrant to get inside." Miles's gaze was thoughtful. "Although without much to go on, I'm not sure the judge will grant it."

Paige didn't say anything, sensing that Abby was still listening to their conversation. The last thing she wanted to do was to scare her little girl any more than she clearly already was. Yet she didn't think they'd find Travis in his condo. For one thing, there were people living on either side of him who would have called the police if they'd heard any kind of commotion going on.

Plus, if there was any connection between Travis being on ChatTime with Abby and the subsequent shooting, there hadn't been enough time for anyone to get from Travis's condo to her house. His condo was located a good thirty minutes away.

But what if Travis had been closer? Like, almost to her house when he'd connected with Abby? It didn't seem likely that he'd bother talking with his daughter from his car, unless... A stab of fear hit hard.

Unless connecting to ChatTime had been an accident?

"There must be somewhere else that Travis might go," Miles persisted, interrupting her thoughts. "He must have some sort of hobby."

"Women."

Miles blinked. "Excuse me?"

She pressed her lips together in a firm line. "The only hobby Travis has is going out with women. Fidelity isn't his strong suit."

Miles winced as he realized that explained their divorce. Paige deserved so much better than a man who would cheat on her. "Do you know who he's seeing now?"

Paige let out a harsh laugh. "I caught a glimpse of a tall blonde the last time I saw him, but the way he goes through women, I wouldn't bank on the possibility she's still in the picture. He likes them pretty and brainless."

"Abby?" Miles gave her daughter a gentle smile. "Do you know the name of your daddy's girlfriend?"

The little girl shook her head and Paige let out a sigh of relief. She'd encouraged Travis not to introduce a string of women to Abby and it seemed like he might have actually honored her request for once.

Then again, he hadn't been alone with Abby for the past six weeks. She frowned, thinking back to when she'd last seen Travis. Maybe three weeks ago? Yeah, that was it. She'd driven to Sci-Tech because his child support check had been late. Travis had come out to meet her in the parking lot to give her the payment and the tall, beautiful blonde had accompanied him. As soon as he'd given her the check, the two of them had headed to his car, obviously going out on a date.

Had he introduced them? She never paid much attention, unsure why Travis felt the need to show off his latest girlfriend. Each time he did that, she was reminded about how glad she was that he was no longer her husband. Yet he was still Abby's father...

Then it came to her. "Sasha." At the surprise in Miles's eyes, she clarified, "The blonde's name was Sasha. Sorry, but I don't think he gave me a last name. Or if he did, I didn't pay any attention."

"Great. At least it gives us someplace to start."

She brushed strands of damp hair away from Abby's face, grateful to note that the little girl's body had relaxed, the earlier fear of the computer seeming to have vanished. "Let's get some sleep first, okay?"

Abby lifted her head and gestured to the bathroom. Paige understood and helped Abby down from the bed. Taking her hand, Paige helped her to use the bathroom then wash up. Abby drank a full cup of water before she turned and opened the bathroom door.

The lamp was still on in the corner, but Miles's computer wasn't anywhere to be found. He was sitting on the side of the bed, finishing up a phone call, as they emerged.

"Learn something new?" she asked when he glanced over at them.

"Not yet."

She couldn't help wondering if he'd tell her, even if he had a lead. From what she saw on TV, the police never wanted to talk much about their investigations. She tucked Abby into bed and sat down beside her.

"Let's say our prayers, okay?"

Abby looked up at her and placed her hands together. But she didn't speak, so Paige recited the bedtime prayer in a low voice. When she finished, Paige leaned over and pressed a tender kiss to Abby's cheek.

"I love you."

Abby didn't say the words back, the way she normally would, but she did kiss her cheek. Paige's eyes went misty as Abby grabbed Ellie beneath her arm and snuggled into the covers.

"Sweet dreams," Paige murmured.

A faint smile flickered on her daughter's face as her eyes drifted closed. Paige gazed at Abby's face for several long minutes, amazed at the change in her demeanor since Miles had partially figured out what had frightened her so badly.

Maybe now that at least part of the secret was out, her little girl would be able to find a sense of peace.

And if Abby still wasn't talking in the morning, she'd insist that Miles take her to see a child psychologist to get the help she needed. The detective seemed like a good guy, someone she could count on to do the right thing.

At least, she hoped so.

"Paige?" Miles kept his voice in a low whisper so he wouldn't wake Abby. "Can I talk to you for a minute?"

She looked up at him, then rose to her feet, edging around the bed to come over to his side of the room. There wasn't a lot space, so he backed his chair against the door so she could sit in the chair beside him. She was so close, their knees touched.

"What?" Her eyes were wide behind her glasses. "You think Travis knows something that got that man killed and you're worried about him?"

Yeah, he was, but not exactly the way she thought. Miles cleared his throat. "I hate to ask you this, but could you give me a list of all his girlfriends? At least, the ones you know about?"

She dropped her gaze to the floor, her mouth pressed into a tight line. "It's a long list. I doubt I'd get a tenth of them right."

He hated seeing the self-doubt in her eyes, and wanted to deck Travis Olson for making this gorgeous woman feel as if she hadn't been good enough to keep him. "Anything you can remember would be great. I wouldn't ask if it wasn't important."

"Fine." She picked up a pen and began writing on the motel stationery. After a few minutes she dropped the pen and pushed the note containing five women's names toward him. "These are the only ones I remember."

"Thanks." He folded the note in half and placed it in his shirt pocket.

"Do you think Travis is all right?"

"I'm not sure." He couldn't bring himself to lie to her. "Don't worry, I'll keep looking for him."

"All right, but you're not—leaving us alone to do that, are you?"

One corner of his mouth quirked up. "No, you're stuck with me. Unless you have friends or relatives you'd like to stay with for a few days?"

"Not really. My parents are dead and I'm an only child. I have an elderly great-aunt who lives in Arizona, but she's in one of those senior living apartments and they don't allow kids to stay there." She sighed. "Besides, what if whoever tried to shoot us comes back? I wouldn't want to put anyone else in danger."

He couldn't argue with that logic. "Don't stress, Paige. I'm here for you. We'll figure out our next steps in the morning, okay?"

"Okay." She twisted her hands together in her lap for a moment. "Miles?"

"Yes?"

"Thank you for saving our lives tonight."

The urge to pull her into his arms was strong and he didn't like it. Why was this single mom getting to him like this? He wasn't like Marc, looking to settle down with a wife and family.

Yet there was something about Paige's strength and courage that reminded him a bit of Dawn's battle with cancer. He couldn't help but admire the way Paige cared for her daughter.

He reached out to put his hand over hers, giving a gentle squeeze. "You're welcome. Now try to get some sleep."

She held his hand for a long moment, then stood and made her way back to her daughter's bedside. He switched off the lamp, staring blindly through the darkness.

Miles didn't have a good feeling about Paige's ex-husband and tried to think of where he might be. Hiding out somewhere? Or was it possible

Abby had actually seen something bad happening to her father? It had seemed as if he was getting through to the little girl, and hoped to try again in the morning.

A few hours later, he woke up to a faint light peeking around the heavy curtains. After rubbing the sleep from his eyes, he swung his feet to the floor.

He quickly washed up in the bathroom, and when he came out, he noticed Paige was awake, as well.

"Do you think we could get something for breakfast?" she whispered. "Abby will be hungry when she wakes up."

"Of course." He walked over to where he'd charged up his phone, then moved the curtain aside to check out the parking lot. Everything looked quiet, just the way he liked it. "Let me know when you're ready to go. I'm going to make a few calls."

"All right."

He took the laptop computer outside and stored it in the trunk of his car. Then he stood with his back against the wall so he could keep an eye on the road. There wasn't much traffic on the road yet, probably because it was barely six.

Miles called his captain first, but his boss didn't answer. He left a quick message, then tried Detective Krantz's number. Her phone went straight to voice mail, too.

Obviously it was too early for anyone to be up working. Which only frustrated him more.

He slipped his phone into his pocket and stared at the motel. Staying another night here wouldn't be smart. Even though he knew they hadn't been followed, the break-in at his house bothered him. Why was he suddenly a target, too? For now, it would be best for them to keep moving.

A restaurant serving breakfast that appeared to be family-friendly was located up the road a bit. They'd grab something to eat there, and then decide where to go next. Miles wanted to keep working the case, so he thought about calling his brothers for help in watching over Paige and Abby.

Satisfied to have a plan in place, he went back inside the motel room. Abby was coming out of the bathroom with her pink elephant tucked under her arm.

"Are you hungry?" he asked.

The little girl's eyes brightened and she nodded with enthusiasm.

He glanced at Paige, who shrugged and shook her head. "Abby still doesn't feel like talking."

"That's okay. I'm sure she'll talk when she's ready." At least, he hoped so. "Are you ready to go?"

"Sure," Paige replied, and took Abby's hand. He held the door open, doing another sweep of the parking lot to be sure nothing had changed, before letting the door close behind him.

"I'm parked over here." He led them around the corner to the spot where he'd left his car.

Driving to the restaurant didn't take long, and since the place was totally empty they were seated immediately at a booth overlooking the parking lot.

He and Paige both ordered coffee. Their waitress filled their mugs, then brought a large glass of milk for Abby. Their breakfasts were served just five minutes later.

Paige took Abby's hand and bowed her head. "Thank You, Lord, for this food we are about to eat. And thank You for keeping us safe in Your care, Amen."

"Amen," he echoed, thinking about how long it had been since he'd prayed. Oh, he always attended church with his family, followed by Sunday brunch at his mother's house, but generally he went through the motions without thinking about it.

Yet here was Paige, praying as if she truly meant every word. The way he once had, before Dawn had died. Before he'd lost the woman he'd once loved.

An uncomfortable silence stretched between

them, made worse by Abby's muteness. He was glad to see that she was at least eating her French toast drowned in maple syrup and the side of bacon. Thankfully, whatever was keeping her silent wasn't bad enough to interfere with her appetite.

"Where do we go from here?" Paige asked when she'd finished her meal.

"Another motel would be best."

She wrinkled her nose. "Couldn't we stop back at my house to pick up some things? Clothes, toiletries?"

He didn't want to take her back there, but he understood she needed something more than just the clothes on their backs. He'd stashed a spare pair of sweats for her in his duffel, but he didn't have anything for a child. "I'll get you both settled in a motel closer to town and I'll get one of my brothers to pick up some things for you, okay? You can give me a list."

Their waitress set their bill on the table, and he took out enough cash to pay the tab and leave a tip. When he glanced up, a movement outside caught his attention.

A black sedan with tinted windows was rolling way too slowly past the restaurant.

The hairs on the back of his neck lifted in alarm. His navy blue car was parked next to a bright yellow Chevy truck, but it wasn't as if his vehicle was hidden from view.

The black car stopped, then backed up about a foot as if to get a better angle to see the license plate.

Miles didn't like it. "Come on, we need to go. Now."

Paige followed his gaze outside, then paled. "What's wrong? Do you recognize that car?"

"No." Even as he spoke, two men slid out of the vehicle, wearing black from head to toe, their eyes covered by dark glasses. And he could tell by the bulk beneath their clothes, they both were carrying guns.

"This way, hurry!" He scooped Abby into his arms and tugged Paige's hand. The waitress gaped at them, as he headed toward the kitchen.

"Hey, you can't go back there!"

"Call the police," he said tersely, brushing past the swinging doors to the kitchen. He knew there would be a back door leading outside, and he wanted to get as far away from the armed men as possible.

"Stop! You can't be back here!" The cook, a large man with a receding hairline protested when Miles wove through the shiny metal tables and shelves.

Miles ignored him but the yelling obviously bothered Abby because she hid her face against his neck. He gave the little girl a brief, reassuring hug, then handed her over to Paige.

"I'm going outside first, you stay back until I tell you it's clear."

Paige nodded, her eyes frightened, but calm, as if she were just as determined as he was to get away.

There was a large Dumpster out back, and a few yards ahead were three evergreen trees. Using the Dumpster for cover, he peeked around the edge so he could see.

One of the two men was standing near his car, pointing toward the bullet hole. The other wasn't in view, and Miles suspected they'd head inside the restaurant any moment.

"We have to move, now! Toward the trees." Miles urged Paige to go first, so that he could provide cover. "Hurry."

They made it to the cluster of trees but from there, wide-open fields stretched for what looked like a half mile. A white farmhouse in the distance provided the only possible source of cover.

"See that farmhouse?" he asked. Paige nodded. "We'll have to make a run for it."

"But it's so open," she protested.

She was right, but there was a small pile of rocks not far from the cluster of trees. Miles thought he could stretch out on the ground behind the rocks and provide cover, shooting at the men to keep them at bay, while Paige and Abby ran to safety.

But he didn't have a chance to outline his plan because the back door of the restaurant burst open and shots rang out.

FOUR

With her heart pounding frantically, Paige clutched Abby to her chest, shielding her daughter as best she could as she hid behind the evergreen trees. Miles pushed her behind him, then squatted in front of her and returned fire.

The gunshots were excruciatingly loud, making her ears ring, and she knew they frightened Abby, too, by the way her daughter's tears dampened her shirt. Paige had no idea why these guys were shooting at them and prayed the waitress had, indeed, called the police.

The sharp scent of cordite hung in the air. Miles fired twice more, and she caught a glimpse of two men lying on the ground in front of the door. She couldn't tell if they were alive or dead. Then Miles was hauling her up to her feet. "Come on, we have to get out of here."

She wasn't about to argue. She wanted to get as far away from this place as possible.

"Head for my car." Miles urged her forward,

indicating she should go first. She darted around the Dumpster, then sprinted as fast as she could across the parking lot to his car. Just like the night before, she yanked open the passenger door and quickly crawled into the back, unwilling to let Abby go.

Miles shut the passenger door behind her, then ran around to the driver's seat. Before getting into the car, though, he went down to where the black sedan was parked to peer at the license plate. It only took a few seconds, but she found herself holding her breath until he joined them.

He slid behind the wheel, then floored the gas pedal, tires squealing as he drove away from the restaurant. The sound of sirens sounded faintly, as if the police were still far away.

"Who were those men?" She forced the words past the lump in the back of her throat. "Are they the same ones who shot at my house? And if so, how did they find us?"

"I don't know." His expression was grim as he met her gaze in the rearview mirror. "They had handguns, not a twenty-two rifle, so I can't say for certain they're the same ones who shot at your house. But one thing is for sure, the guy I watched obviously recognized my car. We need to get a new set of wheels, ASAP."

Paige tried to rein in her scattered thoughts. "How would they recognize your car?"

Miles shook his head, keeping his gaze focused on the road. "Maybe from last night, when I drove away from your house. It's possible they caught my license plate number. One of the gunmen pointed to the bullet hole in the rear fender."

She couldn't wrap her mind around it. "So now they'll kill you, too? Just to get to me and Abby?"

Miles didn't say anything and she couldn't blame him.

He was in grave danger now, too, because of her.

Miles mentally repeated the license plate number until it was embedded in his memory. The wailing sirens grew louder so he made a sharp left, hoping he was heading in the opposite direction. He didn't want to stop long enough to talk to cops in a different jurisdiction, not when he knew that whoever was behind the attempts to kill Paige and Abby knew what car he was driving.

Did Sci-Tech have access to the DMV database? Maybe. He quickly called his brother, Mitch. "Yeah?" his brother sounded groggy, as if Miles had woken him up. Granted it was only seven thirty in the morning, but still.

"We were ambushed not far from the motel. I need your help getting a spare set of wheels."

"Are you okay?" After Miles quickly filled him in, he went into typical Callahan problem-solving mode. "You want to borrow my buddy, Garrett's, truck?" Mitch asked. "He's still in Afghanistan."

Miles hesitated, wondering if the connection was too close. A few months ago, his older brother, Marc, had borrowed Garrett's truck, and the bad guys had still found him.

Then again, in Marc's case the bad guy had been in law enforcement with easy access to information about Marc and the Callahan family, not part of some high-tech corporation.

"Yeah, that would work, at least for now," he agreed. "But I also want new phones and another safe place to stay."

"Where are you now?" Mitch asked. "I'll come and meet you wherever you want."

Miles squinted at the road sign. "Looks like I'm about fifteen minutes outside of Brookland. Why don't we meet at the park-and-ride right off the interstate?"

"Sounds good. I'll be there." Mitch disconnected from the call.

"Who is Mitch?" Paige asked.

"One of my brothers." He met her questioning gaze in the rearview mirror. "Mitch is an arson investigator, so he understands what it's like to be in danger and why we need a different set of wheels."

"How many brothers do you have?"

He sensed she was making small talk in an

effort to calm her daughter. "Four brothers and a sister, there's six of us altogether. Don't worry, we can trust them."

She nodded, her lips curving in a slight smile as she pressed a kiss against Abby's head. "Having a large family sounds nice."

He thought about the fighting and bickering they'd done as they were growing up, wondering how their parents had put up with them. Yet Paige was right. Looking back, he realized he wouldn't have it any other way.

"We're safe now, Abby," she said in a low, husky tone. "We're going to get a different car and find a new place to stay."

As usual, Abby didn't respond, at least not verbally. Miles wished he could get the little girl to open up so he could find out what she had seen over the ChatTime link. Something about her father, but what? Had he called to talk to Paige, but been interrupted? Miles couldn't imagine her father had attempted to give important information to a child.

He saw the glossy red truck waiting for them in the commuter parking lot and headed in that direction. Mitch eased out from behind the wheel when Miles approached.

"Hey," his brother greeted him. "The disposable phones are in the passenger seat."

"Thanks." Miles pushed open the driver's side

door, then opened the passenger door for Paige and Abby. "Paige, this is my brother, Mitch Callahan. Mitch, this is Paige Olson and her daughter, Abby."

"Nice to meet you." Paige shifted Abby in her arms so that she could offer her hand.

"Same goes," Mitch replied. He smiled at Abby. "Hi, Abby. How old are you?"

Abby hid her face against Paige's neck and Miles scrubbed his hands over his face, knowing that exchanging gunfire with the two thugs behind the restaurant had no doubt shaken the little girl's faith in his ability to keep them safe.

"It's been a rough twenty-four hours for her," Paige said softly.

"For you, too," Miles added. "We barely managed to get away from the last pair of gunmen. I'm hoping that using the truck will cover our trail."

Mitch nodded. "Yeah, no kidding. I went to your place last night. The damage wasn't as bad as I originally thought. Whoever searched the place didn't break stuff, but they sure looked in every nook and cranny. What do you think they were after?"

"I have no idea," Miles replied, scrubbing a hand wearily over his face. He had been trying to figure that out for himself, too. The timing being so close to Jason's death and the gunfire at Paige's place made him think that everything was related, especially since he'd been working his father's case for months and hadn't even gotten any clues to go on.

"Work stuff?" Mitch asked.

"No. I don't bring much of that home, and thankfully I had my computer."

"Do you want us to clean the place up for you?" Mitch asked.

"No need to bother. I'll take care of it, later." He opened the passenger-side door for Paige, assuming that carrying Abby around must be exhausting. Her citrusy scent clouded his mind, making him want things he'd planned to avoid, like home and family. "Why don't you sit down? We'll leave in a minute or so."

When Paige couldn't seem to get up, he put his hands around her waist and lifted her, setting her on the seat. Then he went around to the trunk to grab the duffel bag and computer.

"There's a hotel about five miles away, called the American Lodge. The owner is related to a firefighter I trained with and I already smoothed the way for you. They'll take cash, no questions asked."

"Great, thanks." Miles slapped his brother on the back. "I owe you."

"Nah, this is what family is for, right?"

Miles nodded, then tossed his brother the keys to his car. "Don't use it for long, leave it at my place."

"I will. Mike is going to pick me up there, after we take another look through, make sure there isn't anything that was missed."

Miles highly doubted that the people who'd searched his home left anything behind, but he understood his brother's desire to help out. "Thanks, bro. I'll be in touch."

The ride to the American Lodge didn't take long, and he was surprised to see there was a church located nearby. For the first time since Dawn's death he found he was interested in actually attending a service.

But not until he knew for certain they'd be safe.

The motel room seemed larger to Paige than the one they'd stayed in the previous night, although having additional space didn't matter much, not when Abby still clung to her, as if afraid to let go.

She eased down on the edge of the bed. "Look around, sweetie, isn't it nice here?"

Abby didn't answer, not even by shaking her head.

She lifted her troubled gaze to Miles. "She's been through so much."

"I know." Regret shimmered in his blue eyes and she liked the way he seemed to care about her daughter's well-being.

"I'd like to take her to a child psychologist, but it doesn't seem like an option at the moment."

"I'm sorry, but we can't do that. Not yet."

Although she hated it, she understood. "Would you like to watch a movie?" Paige nodded toward the television and Miles brought the remote over for her. But when she turned on the television and found the kid's channel, Abby didn't even look at the screen.

Paige swallowed hard, trying to figure out what to do to get through to her daughter. After turning off the television, she gently rubbed her hand down Abby's back.

"Let's pray, okay, Abby?"

"Good idea." To her surprise, Miles came over and sat down beside her. He placed one hand at her waist and the other hand on Abby's back. "Dear Lord, we thank You for protecting us today," he said.

It took her a minute to pick up the thread of the prayer. "We ask You, Lord, to continue looking after us, keeping us safe from harm."

"We ask this in Your name, Christ the Lord, Amen."

"Amen," Paige echoed, humbled by how willing Miles was to pray with her, even if only for Abby's sake. Something Travis had refused to do.

When Abby turned her head and looked toward Miles, Paige hoped that she was finally ready to talk, but instead her daughter reached out and patted Miles on the arm, as if thanking him for being there.

Tears burned her eyes, and she quickly tried to blink them away before Miles could see them.

He picked up Abby's hand and gave it a brief kiss. "I promise to protect you and your mom, okay?"

This time Abby nodded.

"Will you watch a movie with your mom?"

Abby nodded again, and Paige let out a little sigh of relief. Her daughter still wasn't talking, but at least she was responding.

To Miles.

She turned the television back on and Abby finally relaxed her grip. Paige plumped up the pillows and eased Abby against them, making sure that Ellie was nearby.

Amazing that Ellie had made it this far, considering everything they'd been through.

"Do you want to make a list of things you need from your house?" Miles asked in a hushed voice. "As I mentioned before, I'll ask one of my brothers to head over there to pick up whatever you need."

While she wasn't thrilled with the thought of some strange man going through her personal things, she desperately wanted a change of clothes and more toys for Abby. Keeping a child occupied in a hotel room wasn't easy. "That would be nice, thanks."

"It's the least I can do," Miles said with a frown. "I feel terrible that those guys managed to trace my car."

"It's not your fault," she protested. Taking the paper and pen from the desk, she quickly wrote out a list of items that she'd love to have. "Here you go."

Miles took the list. "As soon as the disposable phones are charged and ready to go, I'll call my brother, Mike. He's a private investigator, and I'm sure he'll be able to get in and out of your place without anyone detecting him."

"Speaking of phones, I'd like to call my boss," Paige said. "I normally work from home, and he'll wonder why I'm not logged in to my email."

Miles lifted a brow. "What type of work?"

She straightened her glasses and suppressed a sigh. There was no getting around the fact that her job was dull and boring. "I'm an accountant."

"Nice, I'm impressed," Miles said, admiration clear in his tone. His smile of approval warmed her heart. "Numbers aren't my strength."

"Numbers make sense, at least most of the time."

"What company? It's nice that your boss lets you work from home."

"I work for Larson and Avery, they're a group that supports several small businesses." She dragged her fingers through her hair, thinking about what to say to convince her boss to give her a few unplanned vacation days. "I like it a lot better there than Sci-Tech."

"What?" Miles snapped his head around to stare at her in shock. "You used to work at Sci-Tech as an accountant?"

"Yes. Why?" she replied, confused by his reaction. "It was several years ago. I left shortly before my divorce, knowing I needed a more flexible schedule, and Sci-Tech made it clear that working from home wasn't an option."

"Did you have access to sensitive information while you were employed there?" Miles pressed. "Something that would cause them to come after you?"

It took a minute for her to figure out what he meant. "Not at all. I handled their purchasing and accounts receivables, nothing related to payroll or anything like that." She couldn't believe Miles would think that the gunmen had come after her because of her old job.

"What sort of supplies did they purchase?"

She wrinkled her nose. "Nothing exciting, trust me. Lots of computer parts, mostly, some robotics. I only handled the smaller accounts…my boss handled the bigger clients."

"Do you know if Sci-Tech had any government contracts?"

"If they did, my old boss, Steve Kane, would have been the one who worked on them, not me."

"Yeah, okay."

"This," she waved her hand in the air, "isn't related to my work at Sci-Tech. Why would it be? I've been gone for a long time. There's no reason for anyone there to worry about what I might have stumbled across, especially now."

"You're probably right," Miles agreed. "I was just surprised to find out you once worked there." He was silent for a moment before asking, "You're sure you didn't know Jason Whitfield?"

She slowly shook her head, thinking back to the time when she'd been employed at Sci-Tech. "I'm sure. I didn't associate with the tech team who worked for Travis. Our marriage was rocky even back then, so I avoided contacting him at work. I'm sorry. I wish I could help."

"It's okay. I just needed to be sure."

She nodded, wondering again about Travis. She wanted to ask Miles about her ex but hated to bring up the subject in front of Abby. Especially since her daughter was finally relaxed enough to watch a movie.

Was Travis still missing? Or was he simply off somewhere with his latest girlfriend? She hoped the latter, because Abby had been through enough and losing her father might send her over the edge.

The phones took almost an hour to charge and activate. Miles handed her one phone, keeping the other for himself. "I programmed my number into your phone and vice versa."

"Thanks." She moved to the opposite side of the room, hoping to minimize the background noise as she made the call to her boss. Greg wasn't happy about the fact that she needed a few days off work, but in the end he gave in.

She disconnected from the call, feeling relieved to have that task finished. Slipping the phone into her pocket, she climbed up on the bed beside Abby, listening as Miles contacted his brother, giving Michael the list of things she'd requested from the house.

Miles opened his laptop computer, turning it so that the screen wasn't facing Abby. Paige watched him work for several minutes, admiring his handsome profile.

Don't, she warned herself, dragging her gaze away and giving herself a mental shake. Miles was her self-appointed protector, nothing more. He was a nice guy who'd gone out of his way to connect with her daughter. Truthfully, she was glad Abby wasn't afraid of him.

He treated her daughter better than her own father did.

She closed her eyes, ashamed of her thoughts. Travis tried to be a good father, even if he didn't spend as much time with Abby as he should.

But she highly doubted he'd ever prayed with Abby, the way Miles had.

Enough. Once Miles found Travis and figured out who had been shooting at her house, and why, she'd never see Miles again. Which was fine with her.

She wasn't beautiful, not like the women Travis went out with. And she absolutely didn't need a man in her life. Taking care of Abby, personally and financially, was already a full-time job.

Her daughter was her life. She refused to do anything to disrupt that.

Miles let out a low whistle, breaking into her thoughts. "What? Did you find something?" she asked.

He nodded, staring at the computer screen.

She slid off the bed and crossed over to look at what he'd found. The words Sci-Tech, Inc. were on the screen.

"I don't understand," she said with a frown.

"I looked up the license plate of the black sedan from the restaurant," Miles said, his expression grim. "The sedan is registered to Sci-Tech."

She sucked in a harsh breath as the reality of

what she was seeing sank into her brain. "They sent gunmen after us?" she asked in a strained whisper.

"Yeah, that's what it looks like."

She shivered. If the gunmen were employed by Sci-Tech, then it was no small leap to assume Travis was in danger, too.

If he was even still alive.

FIVE

The color drained from Paige's face, causing Miles to mentally kick himself for sharing this with her. "Sit down," he said in a gruff voice, tugging her arm toward the chair beside him. "I didn't mean to scare you."

"Travis," she whispered. "They're after me because of him, aren't they?"

"I think so, yes." He reached over and cradled her icy hands in his. "I'm sorry."

She gripped his hands tightly. "You have to find him, before it's too late."

He didn't want to point out that it might already be too late. Whatever Abby had seen on the tablet had frightened her to the point she wouldn't speak. Had Travis told her to keep quiet? Or had she seen something horrible? He found himself hoping for the first option, but feared the latter.

"I'm not sure where to look for Travis," he admitted. "There's no way to know where he'd go to hide if he thought he was in danger."

"Did you give the police the list of names I gave you?" Paige asked. "I know they're only a few names, but…" Her voice trailed off as if she knew how impossible it would be to find any of Travis's girlfriends.

"I've been searching on their names, especially Sasha, since it's not as common as the others, but I haven't found anything yet." He hated having to disappoint her. "At least we have another link to Sci-Tech. No wonder they were stonewalling me."

Paige nibbled on her lower lip. "I might be able to get inside the building," she offered.

"No." His knee-jerk reaction surprised him, and he tried to backpedal. "I mean, if they're the ones behind this, then it's not safe for you to go there. Besides, how would you get in?"

She lifted her uncertain gaze to his. "I know a couple of the security guards pretty well. If I waited until after hours, when there's only one security guard manning the desk, I might be able to convince them to let me in."

"I know you want to help, but it's not worth the risk." He couldn't stand the idea of Paige walking into the equivalent of the lion's den. "You don't know for sure which security guard would be on duty. And, besides, if anything happened—Abby would be lost without you."

She blinked, and he thought he saw the glint of

tears. "Logically, I know you're right, but it's hard to sit back and do nothing, without even trying."

"I'll find a way to do something, while keeping you and Abby safe." He couldn't stand the thought of her worrying about things she couldn't change. He'd protect her, no matter what. "However, there is one thing you can do."

She lifted her gaze to his. "What's that?"

He stared at her for a moment, struck by her wholesome beauty. She wasn't striking in the way some women were, but he liked the way she didn't wear much makeup and he thought she looked cute in her glasses.

He pulled himself away from that train of thought, knowing it would lead nowhere good, and forced himself to let go of her hands. "Tell me what you know about Sci-Tech's competitors." The black sedan being registered to them had given him an idea. "There must be other companies that are working on similar projects."

"ACE Intelligence, Inc.," she said without hesitation. "They've been in the market for at least ten years, maybe longer, and I know that Sci-Tech was hoping to bring some new technology to market before they did."

"Where are they located?" Miles was already typing the company name into the search engine of his computer.

"North of Chicago. ACE are initials of the owner, Aaron Connor Eastham."

He found the location of the competition; it was only fifty miles from Milwaukee. "Do you think anyone from Sci-Tech used to work at ACE?"

"I have no idea," Paige said with a resigned sigh. "I worked in a cubicle located near the other business offices. I was about as far from the real work being done there as you could get."

He stared at the computer screen, his thoughts whirling. He tried to think back over what Jason had talked about the last time they'd been together, but he couldn't remember anything specific. His buddy had been stressed—Miles remembered there had been a tic near the corner of Jason's left eye that had never been there before. But when he'd pressed the other man for more information, he'd only mentioned that his boss, Travis Olson, was making life miserable at work.

Miles couldn't remember Jason mentioning anything about ACE Intelligence or any other competing company causing concern.

His phone rang, and he warily answered. "Callahan."

"It's me," Mike said. "I have the stuff from the Olson house and I'm here in the parking lot. I didn't want to cause alarm by knocking."

"We're in room 7. I'll unlock the door." Miles rose to his feet and flipped the dead bolt back, then unhooked the chain. When he opened the door, he could see his brother walking across the parking lot, rolling a medium-sized suitcase.

"Moving in?" Miles asked dryly, as he took the suitcase from his brother and set it inside the doorway.

"Hey, I only brought what you asked for." Mike smiled at Paige. "Nice to meet you, Mrs. Olson."

"Call me Paige." She gave his hand a brief shake, then glanced over at her daughter. Abby's gaze was still glued to the movie and Miles wasn't sure if that was a good sign or not. "That's my daughter, Abby."

"Cute kid." Mike gestured to the suitcase. "Most of the stuff in there is for her."

"I know, thanks."

Miles watched as Paige took the suitcase over to the bed and began to unpack.

"I located the spot where the shooter at the Olson's was standing," Mike said in a low voice. "I found several scrapes on the bark between two trees and I also found a twenty-two shell casing that the uniforms must have missed."

Miles couldn't quite visualize the area. "Which trees?"

"The ones separating her property from the neighbor behind her. Best place to keep an eye on the rear of the house."

"Someone came around the side of the house, then hit my car with a bullet."

Mike scowled. "So there were either two gun-men or the guy in the back slid around to the front."

"There were two guys that came after us at the restaurant," Miles told him. "Could be the same ones. Their car is registered to Sci-Tech."

Mike let out a low whistle. "So, why search your place? Do they think Jason left something there? Did Jason mail you something?"

Miles smacked his forehead. "My PO box."

"What about it?" His brother looked confused.

Miles couldn't believe he hadn't thought of it sooner. "My schedule is so erratic, I rent a PO box at the post office rather than have my mail deliv-ered. If Jason did send me something, it would be at the post office."

"Do you want me to go and check?" Mike asked.

Miles hesitated, wanting to head over there himself. He glanced at Paige, and she must have read his expression because she waved her hand.

"Go ahead. We'll be fine."

He pulled out his keys, his gaze never leav-ing her face. "I won't be gone long, especially if there's nothing important in there."

"I know." Paige's smile was strained, but she

seemed sincere. "Abby's busy with her show, so this is a good time to go."

"I'll keep them safe," Mike promised, patting his shoulder holster so that Miles knew he was carrying. "Just hurry up, okay? I have other things I need to do."

"Thanks." Miles shut the computer then headed out the door to Garrett's truck.

He'd be back before Abby even realized he was gone.

The moment the motel room door shut behind Miles, Paige wanted to run over and open it, begging him not to go. She did her best to swallow her fear and attempted a reassuring smile, so Abby wouldn't become upset.

"Good movie, huh, Abby?" She sat on the edge of the bed, giving her daughter a brief hug.

Distracted by the animation, Abby simply nodded.

Paige had wondered if the constant silence would wear on the little girl to the point where she would finally speak, but so far, that hadn't happened. Of course, running from more gunfire just two hours ago probably hadn't helped.

She stared down at her daughter's soft brown hair, wishing there was a way to seek professional help for her, sooner rather than later. How much damage to the little girl's psyche had already been done? She had no idea but prayed it was only temporary.

Obviously they needed to remain safe, but that didn't mean she couldn't investigate child therapy options.

Miles had left his computer behind, so Paige slid off the bed and crossed over to where Michael was seated. Intently scrolling through his phone, he glanced up in surprise when he realized she was standing there.

"I'd like to use the computer a bit, see if I can find a child psychologist for Abby."

Michael frowned and shoved a lank of hair from his face. He wore his hair longer than Miles and she found herself thinking that while both men were handsome, Miles was far more attractive. He shrugged. "You're welcome to use the computer, but you need to keep a low profile until we find the gunmen."

She glanced over her shoulder at her daughter. "You don't understand. Abby is traumatized. She hasn't spoken a word since all of this started. I need to make sure she's okay."

Michael grimaced. "Trust me, I do understand. I feel bad for your little girl. But think about the fact that the bad guys could try to find you by staking out the child psychologists closest to your home. Or say you did take Abby in for a session, then we have to go on the move again. It's better for you both to wait until this is over."

It hadn't occurred to her that the assailants might try to stake out the child psychologists closest to her home on the chance she and Abby would show up there. The idea made her cringe. Maybe Michael was right, and she needed to wait until the danger passed.

"I'd still like to use the computer." She didn't wait for him to respond, but dropped into the seat and squashed a flash of guilt as she typed in Miles's password, the one he probably didn't realize she'd watched him enter, then used the search engine to research Sci-Tech.

The main number showed up on the computer screen, along with the address. The company wasn't too far from her home—its close proximity had been one of the main reasons she and Travis had purchased the place.

The main number hadn't changed, and she quickly programmed the number for Sci-Tech into her disposable phone. She wanted to call now, but knew it would be better to wait until the end of the day.

Ralph Gerlach was one of the second shift security guards, old enough to be her father, yet he'd always been friendly toward her. Paige had gotten the impression that Ralph might have known something about Travis and his other women and had felt sorry for her. She appreciated Ralph's friendship, too, since most of the staff at Sci-Tech had seemed to avoid her. Being married to the director of Research and Development hadn't worked in her favor. Travis was the kind of boss that most people hated, dictatorial and judgmental, riding his staff hard, pushing them to do better. As a result, that dislike had transferred over to her.

Except with a select few, like Ralph.

If Ralph happened to be scheduled to work today, she might be able to pry a little information out of him. At the very least, she hoped Ralph could tell her the last time Travis had been in to work. Maybe Ralph would also give her an inkling as to what might be going on, like if the upper echelon was worried about anything, like ACE, their largest competitor, or about Travis and Jason.

Something that big would likely find its way down to the frontline staff.

She typed Ralph's name into the online directory, wondering if it was possible he might still have a landline at home. Most people only used cell phones these days, but she knew there were some within the older generation who didn't.

Sure enough, she hit pay dirt and was able to find an address and a phone number for Ralph and Alison Gerlach in the directory. Their home was located within ten miles of Sci-Tech, so she figured there was a good chance she had the right couple. Bypassing Sci-Tech and contacting Ralph at home would be even better.

She entered Ralph's phone number into her phone, then closed the computer and disappeared into the bathroom for some privacy. She called Ralph and was disappointed when the call went straight to voice mail.

After hesitating for a long moment, she disconnected from the line, deciding against leaving a message. The hour was still pretty early. If Ralph had worked second shift last night, he might not be up and about yet.

She'd try again, maybe around lunchtime. And if that didn't pan out, then she'd try calling Sci-Tech after three in the afternoon to see if she could catch Ralph at work.

Paige tucked her phone into the pocket of her jeans, determined to do something in an attempt to help find Travis.

The post office was located about two miles from his home. Miles drove past it, keeping a keen eye on the cars behind him. He hadn't been followed from the motel, but he couldn't deny the slim chance that someone might have picked him up once he'd gotten closer to his place.

Remembering how his home had been thor-

oughly searched made him angry all over again.
The more he thought about it, the more he leaned
toward the theory that whoever had killed Jason
believed Miles knew something. He only hoped
that this trip to the post office wouldn't be in vain.
He wanted, needed to figure out what was going
on to keep Paige and Abby safe from harm.

Somewhere along the line, keeping them safe
was becoming more important than finding the
man responsible for his buddy's death.

After pulling into the small parking lot, he slid
out from behind the wheel of Garrett's truck and
walked inside the building. From what he could
tell no one paid him any attention, but rather than
heading straight for the PO box, he walked over
to the wall where all the postal supplies were sold.
He stood for several long minutes in front of the
various padded envelopes and boxes as if debat-
ing whether to purchase shipping and packing
supplies.

Customers lined up to wait for their turn, and
he subtly watched them for a few minutes, his
cop radar on high alert.

When several customers left and only one more
joined the line, Miles turned away from the shipping supplies and walked over to the rows and
rows of PO boxes. His was one of the larger ones,
big enough for package deliveries, and he found

himself holding his breath as he used the key to access the box.

His jaw dropped in surprise when he saw a thick yellow padded envelope about the size of a paperback novel inside the box. Removing it, his pulse jumped when he realized that the return address was for the house in Madison that he'd once shared with Jason and two other guys while they'd attended college.

No name, just the Madison address.

Jason hadn't lived in Madison after graduation, any more than Miles had. Using their old address was obviously Jason's way of letting Miles know the package was from him. Peering at the date, his gut clenched when he realized the envelope had been postmarked yesterday, the day of Jason's murder. As if his buddy had known that the bad guys were after him and wanted to be sure to leave clues behind for Miles as a precautionary measure.

There was other mail in the box, as well, and he quickly sorted through it, making sure there was nothing else from Jason inside. There wasn't, so he tucked the yellow padded envelope under his leather jacket, hiding it from view, then relocked the box.

Walking slowly outside and along the sidewalk toward the truck as if he didn't have a care in the world wasn't easy. It almost seemed as if he were moving in slow motion while his thoughts raced a mile a minute. What had Jason sent him? He was anxious to find out. Even after he climbed into the truck, he didn't immediately open the envelope, wanting to be far away from the vicinity before he reviewed the contents.

He backed out of his parking space, then left the parking lot, turning right onto Mayflower Drive.

A white four-door sedan pulled in behind him, almost immediately. He kept a steady pace, narrowing his gaze as he peered into his rearview mirror, trying to see if the driver was someone he recognized.

The sun was bright, and the driver wore a baseball cap low over his brow, making it impossible to get a good look at his face. He couldn't even say for sure if the driver was a man or a woman but assumed it was a dude.

Miles told himself that the car pulling up right behind him was nothing more than a coincidence, but as he made several turns, the car remained on his tail. He accelerated. As the car dropped back, he tried to make out the license number, but the front license plate was missing.

Wisconsin state law required a front plate.

Without being too obvious, Miles varied his speed a bit and changed lanes so that he was driving in the center of the three-lane highway. Soon there were a couple of cars between his truck and the white car. He thought about how to best lose the tail, and at the last minute made a left-hand turn as the green arrow changed to amber, then red.

The white car wasn't able to make the turn. Miles gunned the engine, making another left-hand turn, then a right through a strip mall parking lot. Sticking to the speed limit was difficult, every cell in his body screamed at him to hurry, but he didn't want to get pulled over by the police, either.

The white car wasn't anywhere in sight, but Miles still couldn't relax. How had he been found in the first place? Was it possible they'd connected him to Garrett's truck? If so, he needed a new set of wheels, as soon as possible, and not one of his brother's cars, either.

Something without any ties to the Callahan name.

But he didn't dare stop to get a rental car now. For one thing, he didn't want the vehicle in his name, and besides, he needed one of his brothers to help out. Or maybe his sister, Maddy, had a friend who'd be willing to trade vehicles for a while.

Miles drove toward the on-ramp to the interstate, unwilling to waste any more time. He just knew that Jason had sent him something important, hopefully information that would blow the case wide open.

The traffic was light this time of day, and when he saw the white car coming up on his tail, he did a double take. Was it the same car? As the car grew closer he could see that there wasn't a front license plate.

He stepped on the gas, a second too late. There was a loud shot followed by the sound of shattering glass.

The rear window of the truck fell apart into dozens of tiny pieces.

Whoever was riding in the white car was shooting at him!

SIX

Miles ducked down, making himself a smaller target as he pushed the speed limit. One good thing about having Garrett's truck was that the engine had a lot more horsepower than his sedan. He zigzagged between cars, ignoring the blaring horns aimed at him by the other irritated drivers.

He took the first exit and pretty much ran a red light to put more distance between him and the occupants of the white car.

As soon as he was certain he'd lost them, he called his brother Mike. "I've been tailed and shot at."

Mike whistled between his teeth. "Are you okay?"

"Yeah, for now. But I need to lose the tail."

"What do you want to do?"

"I need a new vehicle, ASAP. Any ideas? What about Maddy's old boyfriend, Joey Marchese? Do you think he'd swap vehicles for a while? I feel like we need something that isn't easily linked to the Callahan name."

"I have a better idea," Mike said. "I have an alternate identity that I use sometimes to work cases. I'll use that to rent a car."

"You have a fake ID?" Miles repeated incredulously. "Since when?"

"Since none of your business. You have your job and I have mine. Tell me where you want to meet."

"You'll need to bring Paige and Abby with you," Miles said. "I don't want them left alone."

"Understood."

Miles thought about where they could go to rent a vehicle. "We'd better meet down at the airport…it's large enough that we should be able to get in and out without anyone noticing."

"Okay. I'll meet you there in thirty minutes."

Miles disconnected, dropped the phone in the console between the seats and scrubbed a hand over his face.

That had been a close one, and he wasn't in the clear yet, either. Driving with a missing window would draw attention to him, something he didn't need.

Staying on back roads as much as possible, Miles wove his way toward the airport. When he passed a hardware store, he stopped and purchased duct tape and plastic to cover the open space where the window had once been. He glanced around the parking lot, picking out a truck to swap plates with. He left cash tucked under the wiper blade to make up for his taking the plates, and then quickly swapped them out.

Despite his mitigation strategies, Miles didn't feel very secure as he made his way to the airport. The plastic-covered back window was like a huge red flag waving in the wind, drawing unwanted attention to the vehicle.

When he caught a glimpse of a white car, he backtracked, making sure it wasn't the one that had followed him earlier. It wasn't, and by the time he reached the airport, his anger simmered.

He knew that his friendship with Jason Whitfield had made him a target and he needed to find out why. Miles glanced at the yellow envelope, hoping that it contained the answers he needed.

Whoever had driven the white car had wanted the contents of the envelope, as well. The same people had broken into his house, searching for whatever Jason had sent. At least now he knew for certain that the break-in was connected to Sci-Tech and Jason's murder.

He drove around the long-term parking lot, choosing a narrow spot between two other large vehicles to back into, hiding the broken window from view. Sliding out from behind the wheel, Miles once again tucked the envelope beneath his leather jacket, calling his brother as he walked away from the truck.

"I'm here. Where are you?" Miles asked.

"Coming toward the airport now," Mike confirmed.

"Take the ramp to the right for long-term parking. I'll meet you there." Miles replaced the phone in his pocket and swept his gaze over the area. Thirty seconds later, he saw his brother's nondescript dark green four-door roll into view.

Relieved, he headed in that direction, pausing near the hut where the airport shuttle normally picked up passengers. He quickly jumped into the passenger seat, latching the seatbelt as Mike drove off in the direction of the rental car companies.

"Thanks," Miles said, glancing over at his brother. "I owe you one."

"What happened?" Paige asked from the backseat.

For Abby's sake, he forced a smile, unwilling to scare the child any more than necessary. "Nothing happened. I'm fine. There was a white car tailing me, but I managed to lose it."

Paige's gaze clung to his, mirroring unasked questions. He gave a slight nod, in an attempt to reassure her that he'd fill her in later. She sighed but didn't say anything else.

He hated that he'd made her worry, and reached back to lightly touch her knee. His heart constricted in his chest when she covered his hand with hers for a long moment, before letting go.

Stay focused, he told himself. This wasn't the time to allow his personal feelings to distract him from the case.

Procuring a rental car didn't take long, and Miles was grateful that Mike had gone for an SUV. Paige tucked Abby into the backseat, then closed the door and turned to face him.

"Are you in danger because of me?" she asked point-blank.

"No, none of this is your fault," he said gently, pulling the packet out from under his jacket. "Jason sent me this. I assume it's what they were looking for when they broke into my home."

"The man who was murdered sent that to you?" she echoed in shocked surprise.

"Yeah, on the same day he died."

"What's in there?" Paige's eyes were wide with curiosity.

"I don't know yet." Miles tucked the envelope inside his jacket. "We need to get someplace safe before I go through whatever is in here. But hopefully it will give us some sort of clue as to what's going on at Sci-Tech."

Paige rubbed her hands over her arms, as if she were cold. She didn't say anything more, simply opened the door and climbed into the seat beside her daughter.

Once Mike moved everything from one vehicle to the other, Miles slapped his brother on the back. "Thanks again."

"Sure, no problem." Mike turned away, then glanced over his shoulder. "Try not to wreck this one, okay?"

Miles let out a sigh. "Yeah, I'll do my best." As he drove away from the rental car agency, Miles wondered yet again what Jason had sent that was important enough to kill for.

Paige was irritated with Miles. This mess was hardly his fault, but the fact that he'd left her and Abby alone with his brother, then had been shot at, was unacceptable.

For the first time since Miles had come to her rescue, Paige was forced to admit how much she'd come to lean on him. How much she counted on Miles being there for her and Abby.

What if he'd been killed today?

She stared down at her hands, frowning when she realized they were trembling. Twisting them together helped steady her frayed nerves, at least for the moment.

Miles's voice cut into her troubled thoughts. "Do you want to pick up a booster seat for Abby?"

Paige blinked and looked down at her daughter. The little girl was clutching Ellie under one arm, and one of the dollies that Michael had brought from her house beneath the other. "Yes, that would be nice."

"There's a store up ahead, let me know if you need anything else."

She needed him.

No, wait, she didn't need Miles, not as a potential boyfriend or anything like that. She simply needed him to keep her and Abby safe.

"Nothing I can think of offhand," she managed, hoping her voice sounded normal. She glanced at her watch, keeping an eye on the time. She wanted to try calling Ralph Gerlach again, since he hadn't answered earlier.

"Are you warm enough in that jacket?"

What brought that on? She met his gaze in the rearview mirror. The lightweight jacket wasn't exactly the one she'd wanted Michael to bring from her house, but she wasn't going to complain since the toiletries were more important. Everything else on her list had been for Abby. "It's warm enough. I'll be fine."

Miles frowned, but turned his attention back to the road. Going to the store seemed a bit surreal, as if they were living a normal life, when in fact, nothing was further from the truth.

They all went inside together, Paige holding Abby's hand and Miles opening doors for them. She wondered if other shoppers believed them to be a family. Paige lifted Abby up so she could ride in the front of the cart. Miles hovered close as they went over to the section of the store that displayed car seats.

She picked the same booster seat she had in her car, placing it in the cart.

"Is there anything you want, Abby?" Miles asked.

Abby nodded and pointed, but Paige couldn't figure out what she wanted. "Can you tell me what you want, honey?"

Her daughter scowled and pointed again, more vigorously. As much as Paige wanted Abby to talk, she was hesitant to push too hard, worried she'd end up adding to her daughter's emotional scars. The child still hadn't said a word and Paige was beginning to wonder if she ever would.

"This?" Paige steered the cart toward a display of toys featuring a horse and princess.

Abby nodded her head, reaching out for the toy. The princess was astride the horse, and there weren't a lot of small parts to keep track of, making it the perfect item to keep Abby occupied in the car. Unfortunately, the price seemed a bit steep.

"It's too much. We'll find something cheaper, okay?"

"Don't worry about the price," Miles said in a gruff tone. "I'll take care of it."

"She can't have everything she wants," Paige protested.

"After everything she's been through, I doubt

this one item will spoil her. Consider it a gift from me to her."

Paige thought about the fact that Abby's birthday had come and gone a month ago without any acknowledgment from Travis other than a *Happy Birthday, Sweetie* over the ChatTime link, then acquiesced. "All right, but that's all, understand?"

Abby nodded and hugged the box to her chest, smiling up at Miles in thanks.

"You're welcome," Miles said with a wink, as if she'd thanked him verbally.

Paige suppressed a sigh when Miles stopped at a sale rack full of winter coats and began rummaging through them. "I told you, I'm fine," she insisted.

"They're predicting snow," he said, without looking at her. "How about this one?" He drew out a forest green jacket with a furry hood. "It matches your eyes."

Travis used to call her eyes Irish mud because they were green-gold with streaks of brown. "You're not wearing a blue one," she pointed out, referencing his crystal clear blue gaze.

"No, because black leather is more manly." His eyes crinkled at the corners and she was caught off guard by his teasing.

"If I agree to this, can we check out now?" she asked.

"Of course."

She threw up her hands. "Okay, I'll take it."

Thirty minutes later, they were on their way in the rented car, with Abby safely tucked into her booster seat, playing with the horse/princess toy Miles had purchased for her.

"Are you hungry for lunch?" Miles asked. "We can pick something up and eat at the motel."

"Sure. Abby, are you hungry?"

The little girl nodded.

"What would you like?"

Abby didn't answer and the forlorn expression in the little girl's eyes ripped at her heart.

"Chicken bites?" Paige offered.

Abby perked up and nodded.

She gave Miles their order—Abby's chicken bites and chocolate milk, and a grilled chicken sandwich. He asked for a double bacon cheeseburger, making her smile. Typical man.

The interior of the car smelled like French fries, making her mouth water. She hadn't realized how hungry she was. When Miles pulled up in front of the motel, he glanced over at her.

"Stay here, I'll get our room."

"All right." It wasn't until he was inside the lobby that she remembered her plan to call Ralph Gerlach again. She quickly pulled out her phone and dialed his home number.

After two rings, he picked up. "Hello?"

"Ralph? It's Paige. Paige Olson." She cleared her throat. "I hope I didn't catch you at a bad time?"

"Ah, no, of course not. How are you?" Ralph's voice sounded still and unsure.

"Listen, Ralph, I'm sorry to bother you at home, but I'm worried about Travis. Have you seen him? Has he been at work?"

There was a long pause and Paige gripped the phone tightly, hoping he'd talk to her.

"Mr. Olson hasn't been at work in two days now," Ralph said in a hushed voice, as if he didn't want anyone to overhear. Which was strange, because she'd caught him at home.

"That's odd, are people talking about it?" She pressed. "What are they saying?"

"I don't know. I haven't paid any attention."

She didn't believe him. "Ralph, please. He's Abby's father. I'm worried about him. Tell me what you know."

"I don't know anything," Ralph protested. Then she heard him sigh. "The only rumor I've heard is that the old man fired him."

"Fired him?" Paige repeated with a frown. She hadn't expected that. "For what?"

"I don't know, and I haven't asked," Ralph said. "I'm sorry, Paige, I know you count on his supporting your little girl, but from what I can tell, they've already cleared out his office."

Cleared out his office? She found that odd for some reason. "Yeah, okay. Thanks, Ralph. I appreciate you taking the time to talk to me."

"Take care of yourself and your daughter, Paige."

She disconnected from the line as Miles came out of the lobby. Tucking the phone back into her pocket, she tried to make sense of what Ralph had told her.

If Travis had been fired from his job a few years ago, she wouldn't have been that surprised. It was no secret that his team didn't like him as a leader. But to fire him now, right after Jason was found dead and it appeared Travis had gone missing? The timing was downright suspicious.

Maybe Miles's distrustful nature was rubbing off on her, because she didn't believe it was a coincidence.

Travis may have been fired. Or he may have disappeared, making the owner of the company mad enough to tell everyone he'd been fired.

Travis, where are you?

Had Paige been on the phone? Miles slid behind the wheel, handed her one of the plastic keys, then drove around to the south side of the building where their room was located. He'd asked for something on the first floor in the back, in case they needed to leave in a hurry.

Who would Paige call? No one. He must have imagined it.

After parking the car, he went around to the back to grab the suitcase Mike had brought from their previous motel room. He set the suitcase down, then pulled out his duffel and the laptop computer. The wind was sharp and cold, making him believe the weatherman's forecast of snow might be accurate for once.

After they were settled inside, Miles pulled out the envelope that he'd been dying to look at ever since the moment he pulled it out of his PO box. He barely listened as Paige set Abby up with her food, encouraging her to lean over so she wouldn't spill.

His burger grew cold as he pulled out the thick packet of paper that had been folded in half. He began reading the documents, but it was a bit like attempting to read a foreign language.

Understanding the scientific jargon was nearly impossible, yet he soon figured out that the paperwork outlined a detailed plan that would enable those suffering from spinal cord injuries to walk again.

Wow. Talk about a huge scientific breakthrough.

He glanced up when Paige set his burger in front of him. It took him a moment to realize she and Abby were finished eating and that Abby was once again watching a children's movie. "What did you find out?"

"It's incredible, if it really works." He took a bite of his burger and gestured toward the papers. "I think I figured out what the highly confidential project is that both Jason and Travis were working on."

"Really?" Paige leaned forward, trying to read the small text, her citrus scent permeating his senses.

He filled her in on the gist of what he'd found, wishing she'd sit back and give him some space. Her lemony scent was distracting.

"Amazing," she murmured, her wide green eyes meeting his. "Do you think it's really possible?"

"I have to think it is possible, maybe even probable, since Jason took the time to mail it to me." He took another bite of his food and then flipped through several more pages.

The words *ACE Intel* stopped him cold.

He pushed the burger aside and went back to see what he'd missed. The truth of what he was reading made him sick to his stomach.

"What is it?" Paige reached out and put her hand on his arm. "What's wrong?"

He'd tried to keep his expression neutral, but had obviously failed. "I think—they stole these designs from ACE Intel."

"What?" Paige's voice was a horrified whisper. "No, that can't be right. Travis wouldn't…" Her voice trailed off, her expression turning guilty.

"I think we both know he would." Miles took the papers again, rereading the section. It was clear that they were trying to fix whatever glitch ACE Intel had been unable to work through, in an effort to be the first to bring the technology to market.

"This is why your friend was killed?" she asked. "Money? Fame?"

Miles nodded slowly. "Money is usually the primary reason for all crime. But I'm sure, in this case, fame goes along with it. I wonder how they managed to get the information away from ACE?"

"It had to be someone inside the company." She nibbled her lower lip again, and Miles realized she did that a lot when she was nervous. "I spoke to my friend, Ralph...you know, the security guard I mentioned?"

His gut clenched and he knew he hadn't imagined seeing her on the phone. "You called the company? What if they try to trace the call?"

"No, I called his house. Ralph still has a landline." She grimaced. "Ralph said the rumor going around is that Travis was fired. He claims they've already cleaned out his office."

"Fired?" Call him crazy, but Miles didn't believe it. "Look at these documents. This has clearly been in the works for several years. Why would they suddenly fire him now?"

"I don't know. Maybe they just realized that the idea was stolen."

Miles thought it was more likely that Jason wanted to come clean, the secret eating him alive, and Travis had killed him in order to shut him up.

But, of course, he didn't mention that to Paige. He supposed she could be right, that maybe Travis didn't realize the plans had been stolen, either.

His phone rang, and he recognized Mitch's number. "Hey, Mitch, is something wrong?"

"Yeah. I hate to tell you this, but a body was found in the Milwaukee River and has been identified as Travis Olson. He was murdered, shot in the chest with a small-caliber bullet, just like your buddy, Jason."

When Paige gasped, he realized that she'd overheard Mitch's statement. "Thanks for telling me." He disconnected from the call, dropped his phone and reached out to Paige, taking her into his arms, knowing her worst fears had been realized.

Abby's father—her ex-husband—was dead.

SEVEN

Paige ripped off her glasses, letting them fall to the carpeted floor, and buried her face against Miles's chest, unwilling to let Abby see how upset she was.

Dead. Travis was *dead*.

Deep down, she'd suspected as much, ever since she'd heard that her ex-husband was missing. Yet, as horrible as it was that Travis was gone, she was even more concerned about what on earth Abby must have seen through the Chat-Time link.

Her poor, traumatized little girl. Had she witnessed an attack on her father? Had she seen the face of Travis's killer?

Please, Lord, please help heal Abby!

Miles wrapped his arms around her, holding her close. For the first time in what seemed like forever, she allowed herself to lean on a man, absorbing his strength. Somehow, his musky scent calmed her in a way nothing else could.

She wasn't alone. At least, not today, or tomorrow. Miles would stay nearby until they were safe from harm.

"I'm sorry for your loss," he whispered soothingly, his mouth near her ear.

She swallowed hard past the lump in her throat. "How am I going to tell her?" she sobbed. "I don't even know what she saw that night."

Miles's chest rose and dropped with a deep sigh. "Maybe it's best not to tell her just yet."

Hearing him say the words she'd been thinking made her feel better. "It can't hurt to wait a few days, right?"

"Right." His hand softly caressed her hair and it occurred to her that it had been years since she'd been held by a man. After her disaster of a marriage, she'd avoided any and all relationships.

Trusting a man didn't come easy.

She closed her eyes and tried to gather the willpower to move away from Miles, knowing she shouldn't take advantage of his kindness.

Having her cry all over him wasn't what he'd signed up for when he'd promised to keep them safe.

"Sorry about this. I hope I didn't ruin your shirt," she said, reluctantly pulling away from him. She sniffled loudly and swiped at her face. He was still wearing the dress shirt and slacks from the night he'd rescued her from the gunmen.

Miles tipped her face up, forcing her to meet his gaze. "You have nothing to apologize for, understand? None of this is your fault, Paige. You and Abby don't deserve this."

She tried to smile, but figured it was a weak attempt at best. "You're a nice man, Miles Callahan."

His gaze dropped to her mouth and he grimaced. "Not that nice," he muttered before leaning over to capture her lips with his.

His kiss caught her off guard, but half a second later, she found herself kissing him back, reveling in the warmth and closeness of his embrace.

Until she remembered Abby.

Breaking away from Miles wasn't easy, and she quickly glanced over to make sure Abby hadn't witnessed their kiss. Thankfully, her daughter was still engrossed in her movie, clutching the new horse/princess toy Miles had purchased for her beneath her left arm.

"Yes, you are," she said, as if the kiss hadn't happened. When she noticed the puzzled expression on his face, she clarified, "A nice man. Everything you've done for me, for us, well, let's just say you've treated us better than…" Her voice trailed off as she remembered that Travis would never treat her or Abby poorly ever again.

Miles muttered something harsh beneath his breath, then he rose to his feet. "I need to figure out our next steps," he said in an obvious attempt to change the subject. "Jason's notes aren't nearly as helpful as I'd hoped."

She nodded, reaching up to touch her mouth when he turned away.

Maybe their brief kiss hadn't meant anything to him, but it had to her.

Upsetting to realize she wasn't as immune to the idea of a relationship as she'd wanted to be.

Miles turned away from Paige, wishing he could leave the motel room to gain more than an arm's length of distance from Paige and her adorable daughter. But he didn't dare leave them alone, no matter how much he felt the walls closing in.

What was wrong with him? Why had he given in to the urge to kiss her? Just because he'd thought about how sweet she'd taste didn't mean he'd had to act on it.

Idiot. Now that he'd kissed her, he kept thinking about kissing her again. He could still smell her lemony scent lingering on his clothes. She should have smacked him for taking advantage of her emotional state.

But she hadn't.

He reminded himself he wasn't interested in a relationship. Losing Dawn had convinced him that serious relationships were not for him. Been there, done that. He wasn't going to risk falling in love ever again.

Raking a hand through his hair, he forced himself to concentrate on the investigation. Both Jason and Travis had been murdered, no doubt because of the designs that had been stolen from ACE Intel. But who had stolen them? And why were the gunmen coming after him, Paige and Abby?

He glanced over at the little girl, his stomach clenching with anxiety. The gunmen wanted to silence Paige and Abby because of whatever the little girl had seen through the ChatTime link.

And they were after him because of his friendship with Jason. They were afraid he knew too much.

The black sedan had been registered to Sci-Tech, so that meant that the guy in charge knew that the designs had been stolen from ACE Intel. It was possible they didn't want anyone else to know.

Then why be so blatant about the murders? Why not make the deaths look more like an accident? He walked through the timeline in his mind, thinking about the short time frame between whatever Abby had seen via the link and the gunfire at Paige's house.

How had the gunmen gotten there so fast? Unless they'd been staked out there, for some reason?

He blew out a frustrated breath. It didn't make sense. He was missing something, a key piece of the puzzle.

But what?

He turned around, looking back down at the information Jason had mailed to him. Maybe the answer was within ACE Intel. If he called to talk to the owner…what was his name? Aaron Connor Eastham? Would the guy talk to him about the stolen designs?

It was worth a shot.

Something clutched his leg, and he looked down in surprise to find Abby clinging to him, her face turned up to his, her smile so bright that he couldn't help grinning in return.

"What's up, little monkey?" he asked, reaching down to ruffle her hair.

She pointed at the toy he'd given her.

He frowned. "What happened, did it break?"

She shook her head, pointed again and smiled.

"Oh, I see, you're trying to thank me."

This time she nodded, but she still didn't let go. He hesitated, unsure of what to do next. He threw a helpless glance in Paige's direction. The bemused expression on her face didn't help much.

"Um, you're welcome." He patted the little girl's head again and tried to take a step away. Abby's grip around his leg tightened so that when he moved his leg, she rode along with the motion.

"I think she wants you to pick her up," Paige said with a smile.

"Oh." How did mothers know these things? He reached down and gently pried the little girl's arms away from his leg. She let go and allowed him to lift her up against his chest. Abby wrapped her arms around his neck and gave him a fierce hug.

The gesture was so endearing, he felt his throat grow thick with suppressed emotion. He cherished the moment, thinking that Travis Olson had been a complete idiot for giving up something so precious.

He inhaled the sweet scent of baby shampoo as Abby rested against him, but then she began to wiggle around, indicating she wanted to be put down. With a strange reluctance, he bent over and set Abby on her feet.

Humbled by the little girl's generous trust, he couldn't think of anything to say to break the silence. He found himself praying that God would enable the child to speak again very soon.

He wanted the little girl to be able to put the horror behind her, forever.

"You have a way with kids. You'll be a good father someday."

Paige's comment snapped him out of his reverie. Being a husband or a father wasn't on his agenda, yet he couldn't just blurt that out to her. It was tempting to tell her about Dawn, how watching her die of cancer had made him realize that he needed to live life to its fullest. To do all the things he'd ever dreamed of, before it was too late.

The way Dawn hadn't been able to do all the things she'd dreamed of doing. Oh, sure, he'd given her some great experiences, like parasailing and taking a hot air balloon ride, but time had run out before he could finish their arrangements to go hang gliding.

There were other experiences Dawn hadn't been able to have, either. Traveling abroad and learning to sail...

"I need to make a few phone calls," he said, when he realized Paige was waiting for him to say something. "I'll be right back."

Before she could argue, he scooped up his phone and shrugged into his leather jacket. He walked out of the motel room, closing the door quietly behind him. The frigid March air stole his breath, but helped to clear his head.

He needed to stop thinking about Paige and her daughter as anything other than his job.

His responsibility.

The minute he'd arrested the men responsible for killing Jason and Travis, not to mention shooting at them, he wouldn't see Paige and Abby again. And it was better that way.

For both of them.

Shaking off his disconcerting thoughts, he called Mitch.

"What's up?" his brother asked.

"I want to set up a phone call with Aaron Connor Eastham, the owner of ACE Intel, located north of Chicago. But I need some background information on the guy, first. Do you think you can help me?"

"Yeah, no problem. Give me an hour or so. But what makes you think he'll talk to you?"

"In reviewing the information Jason sent to me, it looks as if Sci-Tech might have stolen scientific intelligence from ACE. I think this guy, Eastham, will have an idea who is behind it."

"Good idea," Mitch agreed. "I'll call you back when I have something."

"Thanks." Miles disconnected from the line just as a light dusting of snow flurries began to fall from the sky.

He swept a glance around the parking lot and didn't see anything that appeared out of place. He felt certain that using Mike's fake ID would help keep them hidden, yet he also knew that there were ways to track someone other than using their vehicle.

He stared down at his phone for a moment, knowing it was well past the time he was ordered to check in with his captain. Resigned, he pressed the numbers into the phone and waited for his superior to pick up.

"O'Dell."

"Captain? It's Callahan."

"Where are you?" his boss thundered. "I should fire you for insubordination!"

Miles winced and did his best to smooth things over. "Listen, I've been shot at twice now, so no matter what you threaten me with, I'm not coming in. Not until I have round-the-clock protection for the woman and her child."

"Who shot at you? When?" O'Dell demanded.

"I don't have time to get into it now. I heard the body of Travis Olson was pulled out of the river with a bullet hole in his chest. He was killed just like Jason Whitfield, and I know for a fact this is all connected to Sci-Tech. I need you to call the DA's office to get a warrant to search Olson's office and his condo."

"Why didn't I think of that?" Heavy sarcasm laced his captain's voice. "It's already in the works. Do you want to be there for the search?"

"Yes." The answer came instinctively, but then he realized that would be impossible. "But I can't."

"I don't recall giving you vacation time," O'Dell said.

Miles closed his eyes, searching for patience. "I'm working another angle. Sci-Tech's biggest competitor is ACE Intel…I'm hoping to interview the owner, soon."

"ACE Intel?" The news mollified his boss. "Where are they located?"

"North of Chicago. I'll let you know what I find out."

"Yeah, you do that." The edge was back in his boss's tone. "Meanwhile I'll send Krantz over to do the search on Olson's office and his condo. Unfortunately the owner of the company is refusing to talk to anyone without his lawyer present."

Apparently the owner of Sci-Tech didn't understand that obstructing an investigation only made him look guilty. "Will you let me know if Detective Krantz finds anything?"

"Yeah, yeah." O'Dell sounded resigned. "Keep in contact, Callahan, you hear me?"

"Loud and clear, Captain." He ended the call and slipped the phone back into his pocket. The snowflakes were melting against his skin, leaving tiny droplets of water behind.

Feeling better about the investigation, he turned to head back inside, summoning the strength to resist getting too close to Paige and Abby.

He needed to bust this case wide open, and soon.

The easy camaraderie that once existed with Miles had been shattered by his kiss.

Not just the kiss, Paige acknowledged, but also since Abby had clung to Miles as if she might never let go.

He hadn't appreciated being told he would be a good father one day, and she didn't understand why her innocent remark had caused him to withdraw from her so completely.

But the fact that it had only proved her point. Miles might be a nice guy, but he wasn't interested in anything more. She'd told herself that before, but now she truly believed it.

The hours seemed to pass with excruciating slowness. Miles had ordered pizza for dinner, which Abby clearly enjoyed.

Paige gave Abby a bath, brushed her hair and then used the blow-dryer to take away the dampness. When they emerged from the bathroom, she was surprised to discover Miles was on the phone, speaking in a low voice.

She couldn't help being annoyed with him for being so secretive. He hadn't shared any details with her of what he had or hadn't learned during his previous phone calls, the ones he'd made while standing out in the cold.

Here he was, doing it again.

"Time for bed," she told Abby. "Ready to say our prayers?"

Abby crawled into bed, pulled her stuffed elephant close then pressed her hands together.

Since it was clear Abby wasn't going to talk, Paige led the prayer. "Dear Lord, we ask for Your blessing as we sleep tonight. Please keep us safe in Your care and continue guiding us on Your chosen path. Amen."

"Amen," a deep male voice echoed from behind her.

Paige glanced over at Miles, surprised he'd joined in with the bedtime prayer. The same way he'd joined them in prayer, earlier. She turned back to her daughter who hadn't said anything.

"Goodnight, Abby," she said, bending over to give her daughter a hug and a kiss. "Sweet dreams, okay?"

Abby nodded and gave her a kiss on the cheek.

When Paige stood, Abby stared at Miles and raised her arms, indicating she wanted to give him a hug and a kiss, too.

Miles glanced at Paige, as if to ask if it was okay. She nodded, and blinked back a ridiculous urge to cry as he bent over to give Abby a cuddle goodnight.

Something Travis hadn't done for a long time. And would never do again.

Miles turned out the light between the two beds, leaving only a small lamp on in the corner of the room. Paige was about to head into the bathroom to wash up, when Miles gently tugged on her arm.

"Do you have a minute?" he whispered.

She nodded and joined him at the small table where he had his laptop computer set up. The papers Jason had mailed to him were scattered around, as if he'd been going over them again.

"What do you know about Karl Rogers?" he asked quietly.

She lifted a brow. "He's the current owner and founder of Sci-Tech."

"Do you know a guy by the name of Lance Anderson?"

She wrinkled her nose. "Lance is Karl's lawyer, and not a very nice man. Why?"

"Karl is refusing to cooperate with the investigation into your ex-husband's death."

"I'm not surprised. Karl and Lance are tight, and I'm sure Lance is advising him to keep silent."

"He does have that right, although remaining silent only makes him look guilty," Miles muttered. "I'm waiting for Eastham to call me back. Do you know anything about him?"

She was glad that Miles was including her in the investigation, but unfortunately, she didn't know anything that might help. "Other than that he's the owner of ACE Intel, I'm afraid not. Travis once mentioned that Karl and Aaron hated each other, which isn't that surprising since they're arch rivals."

you know Jason Whitfield or Travis Olson?"

"No. Why?"

Miles looked at her, as if trying to figure out how much to tell him. She nodded, encouraging him to be up front. "Both men used to work at Sci-Tech, but they've been murdered."

There was a long pause from the owner of ACE Intel, before he asked, "What does that have to do with me?"

"Isn't Sci-Tech your biggest competitor?"

Eastham let out a harsh laugh. "Yeah, but if I was going to go after anyone it would be Karl Rogers, not the people who work for him."

Paige's eyes widened as Miles's expression turned grim. "And why is that?"

"Karl used to work for me, and broke his contract by starting his own business in the exact same field."

...no kidding." His dry tone made her smile.

His phone vibrated and he quickly picked it up. "Hello?"

She leaned close to hear the other side of the conversation.

"Thanks for calling me back, Mr. Eastham. I'm hoping you'll answer a couple of questions for me."

"That depends on what they are," the other man said bluntly.

"Do you h...

now? How...

"Since the day the company op...s."

Paige swallowed hard, not liking the connection.

She didn't want to believe that her ex-husband had been a crook as well as a lousy husband.

EIGHT

Miles resisted the urge to take Paige into his arms, although it wasn't easy. The tears shimmering in her eyes ripped at his heart, he didn't like to see her upset and longed to offer comfort.

But he needed to remain professional. No more kissing, no matter how much he wanted to taste her sweetness again.

"Just because he's been there since the beginning doesn't mean Travis knew anything about the stolen ideas. He still could be an innocent victim in all of this," he pointed out.

She nibbled her bottom lip. "Maybe. But to be honest, Travis was all about fame and fortune. I wouldn't be surprised if he took a shortcut to be the first one to bring something like that to market."

He reached out and lightly touched her arm. "Let's give him the benefit of the doubt, okay?"

Her attempt at a smile made his heart ache. "All right."

"Get some sleep," he encouraged, forcing himself to let go of her arm and sit back in his seat.

"You need to rest, too."

What he needed was to keep them safe, but he nodded. "I'm waiting for a phone call from a colleague."

Paige nodded, then rose to her feet. She looked like she wanted to say something more, but didn't. He watched her disappear into the bathroom and blew out a heavy breath.

Paige and her daughter were getting to him in a way he'd never experienced before. In all of his let's-go-out-and-have-fun relationships, he'd avoided becoming too serious. He hadn't wanted to be overly involved. Obviously being in close proximity to Paige and Abby for the past two days was impacting him more than he'd anticipated.

Focus, he told himself firmly. *On the case, not on Paige.*

He considered calling O'Dell again, but decided against it. Contacting Detective Krantz, though, might work. She was the one executing the search warrant on Olson's office within Sci-Tech and his condo. Although Miles doubted that they'd find anything useful. He wasn't sure when Travis had been murdered, but there had been plenty of time for Karl and his team to get rid of any incriminating evidence if there had been any.

The same held true for Olson's condo.

Miles wondered if Travis had talked about his work with his girlfriends. Not that he'd been able to find any of the women whose names Paige had given him. Working the case from a motel room wasn't impossible, but without last names it was like searching for a shell casing in a forest.

He rose to his feet and made sure he had his key before slipping outside. The snow flurries had stopped but the dark clouds overhead lingered, obliterating any potential light from the moon.

He called dispatch, requesting to be connected with Detective Krantz.

She answered in a curt, no-nonsense tone. "Krantz."

"Detective, this is Miles Callahan. Captain O'Dell told me you're working the Travis Olson case. Do you have any updates you're able to share?"

"Oh, yeah, I heard from O'Dell that you'd be in touch. Let's see." He heard the sound of paper shuffling. "The ME put the time of Travis Olson's death as two days ago, on Monday night."

He frowned. Monday was the same night that Jason had been killed, but he'd thought for sure that Olson had been killed later than that, by twenty-four hours or so. How else would he have connected to Abby through the ChatTime link? Maybe the effects of the water on the body had influenced the ME's time of death. "That's interesting. Anything else?"

"A twenty-two caliber slug was dug out of his chest, same type that killed Whitfield."

That much he'd already suspected, but it was nice to have the evidence confirm his theory. "What about the search warrants? Find anything interesting at Olson's condo or his office?"

"No, we got squat. Hard to tell if he was keeping everything hidden someplace we haven't found yet or if someone else cleaned up behind him."

Probably both, which was exactly what he'd been afraid of. "Listen, I know that the owner of Sci-Tech used to work at ACE Intel, and according to the owner at ACE, Karl Rogers broke a noncompete clause. He managed to avoid any legal issues, though, because Rogers's lawyer came up with a document proving that Rogers was fired, making the contract null and void. I think these two murders are linked to corporate espionage."

There was a brief silence, before Lisa Krantz replied, "Wow, you've been busy. Great work on nailing the motive for murder, Callahan. Where are you? I think it might be better for both of us if we get together and compare notes."

Miles hesitated, then decided it was too late for that since Abby was already asleep. "Maybe tomorrow. But keep me posted on whatever else you might find."

"Sure. What number should I use to contact you?"

"Don't bother calling me. I'll get back in touch with you when I'm able. Good night." Miles disconnected from the call, belatedly realizing that he'd forgotten to fill Krantz in on the information Jason had sent to his PO box. He briefly considered calling her back, then decided that there would be time to fill her in tomorrow.

He walked the length of the motel, taking note of the different vehicles parked back there. Standing beside the rental SUV, Miles decided to move it farther down from their room, and to back it into the parking space, just in case they needed a quick escape.

They should be safe here, but he couldn't quite get rid of the nagging worry that plagued him. Being responsible for a witness was rough enough, but adding a woman and a five-year-old child to the mix added another level of pressure.

Before getting out of the SUV, he removed the bulb from the dome light. Paranoid? Yeah. But better that than dead.

He made one more sweep around the building before using his key card to unlock the door. The interior of the room was dark, with the exception of a sliver of light beneath the bathroom door.

After waiting a moment for his eyes to adjust to the darkness, he carefully made his way toward the door. A glance at the bed confirmed that Paige wasn't there.

Listening at the bathroom door, he was able to hear her crying. Not loudly, but soft hiccuping sobs that ripped at his heart.

Normally, he avoided crying women, but he couldn't make himself walk away. Instead, he braced his palms on the sides of the door. "Paige?" He whispered, to avoid waking Abby. "Are you all right?"

The crying grew quieter, as if she were trying to rein in her emotions. "Fine." The word was hoarse, as if she'd been sobbing for a while. "Go to sleep."

Yeah, right. Not hardly. "Open up," he urged.

There was a long pause, then the sound of running water. He imagined she was trying to minimize the evidence of her tears. The seconds stretched into one minute, then two, before the door opened.

"I'm fine," she repeated. Her gaze was downcast, and it hurt to realize she didn't want to look at him.

"Oh, Paige," he murmured, reaching out to draw her against his chest. "Don't cry. Everything will turn out okay, you'll see."

She held herself stiff for a moment, then finally

relaxed against him. "I'm sorry," she whispered. "I don't know what's wrong with me. Usually I'm stronger than this."

"You're one of the strongest women I know," he told her honestly, thinking again of how much she reminded him of Dawn. Yeah, there were some differences. His college sweetheart had been fighting for her life, while Paige was fighting for her daughter.

He admired Paige for that. For putting Abby first.

"Thanks." Paige pulled out of his arms and swiped again at her face. "Goodnight, Miles."

He forced himself to take a step back, when all he really wanted to do was to kiss her again. *Bad move*, he reminded himself. *Not smart to get personally involved.*

She scooted around him and crawled into bed beside her daughter. He used the bathroom and shut off the light when he was finished.

He didn't bother going to bed, though, knowing sleep would elude him.

Not only because he was worried about the gunmen finding them once again, but because he knew, deep down, he was in trouble.

Despite his efforts to the contrary, he was already emotionally entangled with Paige and her daughter.

* * *

Paige closed her eyes, willing herself to fall asleep. She was mortified that Miles had witnessed her breakdown, even though he'd been so sweet about it. Being held in his arms had soothed her but she'd already leaned on him far more than she had a right to.

She wasn't even sure why she'd started crying in the first place. Travis was gone, but her marriage had been over a long time ago. And it wasn't as if Travis had been there for Abby over the past few years, either. At the time of their divorce, she'd been glad that he hadn't fought for custody. Now she wished that her daughter would have better memories of her father, other than whatever she'd witnessed during the ChatTime link.

It was sad to think of the relationship Abby would never have with her father. A less-than-involved father was better than having no one at all, wasn't it? Paige had been blessed to have both her parents until they passed away, each from a different kind of cancer.

She flipped onto her side, being careful not to jostle her sleeping daughter. The room was claustrophobic, maybe because she was hyperaware of Miles being nearby, but somehow she managed to fall asleep.

A muffled thump woke her, and she blinked groggily in the darkness, trying to figure out what she'd heard. It took a few minutes for her to real-ize that the lump in the other bed was Miles. Like her, he was dressed and covered with a blanket, as if ready to leave at a moment's notice.

She heard the thump again and figured the noise must be coming from people in the room next door. Slipping out of bed, she padded over to the window, peeking through the curtains to the parking lot outside.

A pair of headlights flashed as a dark car drove slowly past the row of cars parked in front of the building. The tiny hairs on her arms prickled with unease. The dark car looked similar to the one that had found them at the restaurant the previ-ous morning.

She told herself there were many dark cars and there was no reason to think this was the same one. She'd read somewhere that black was one of the most popular colors for new cars.

If it wasn't the same one, why was it moving so slowly?

Paige crossed over and gently shook Miles's shoulder. He shot upright and she swallowed a squeak of alarm at how instantly he became awake. "What's wrong?"

"Come look at this," she whispered when she'd found her breath.

"What?" Miles didn't hesitate, but swung his legs over the edge of the bed and stood.

"There's a dark sedan outside."

He moved into position at the window, peering intently through the gap in the heavy curtains.

"All I see are taillights." He turned toward her, a frown furrowing his brow. "But it's moving slower than you'd expect from someone renting a room."

She gripped his arm, partially because her knees felt weak. "Is it possible the gunmen have found us again?"

"Unfortunately, anything is possible." Miles turned back toward the window and she wondered if she'd let her imagination get the better of her.

"It's probably nothing," she whispered. "Sorry I woke you."

Miles stood there for several seconds before leaning toward her. "I'm going to check around outside. Stay here with Abby, okay?"

She nodded. "Don't be gone too long."

"I won't. The car is probably gone by now, anyway, or maybe the driver was having trouble finding a spot to park near his room. I'm sure it's nothing, but we'll both sleep better if I double check." He drew on his shoulder holster and covered the weapon with his black leather jacket. He eased the door open and disappeared soundlessly into the night.

Paige walked over to make sure Abby was still sleeping, then pulled a chair near the window to wait, hoping that Miles was right and that there was nothing to worry about.

Yet the way her stomach was churning, she suspected otherwise.

The moment Miles closed the door behind him, he pulled his weapon and dropped into a crouch, using the parked cars in front of the motel as cover.

The building had rooms along the front and along the back, and he couldn't tell for sure if the vehicle Paige had noticed was still circling the building or if the driver had chosen a parking spot.

It didn't make sense that the gunmen would find them here. The only people he'd spoken to were his boss and Detective Krantz. Using a throwaway phone made tracking him that much more difficult.

Difficult, but not impossible. If someone had the right connections...

No, he didn't believe he'd been traced here through a phone call to the police station. In fact, the dispatcher had sent his call to Krantz's phone and he knew that meant she didn't have his number.

Only his boss, Captain O'Dell, had it. And O'Dell had been on the force for twenty years. Miles trusted the man with his life.

But with Paige and Abby's? Not so much.

Then again, Paige had also called that security guard.

He moved stealthily from one car to the next, listening for sounds of a car engine. He turned and was almost back at their motel room door when he heard it.

The car had returned, once again moving suspiciously slowly. Maybe it was his imagination, but it looked as if the occupants were checking each and every license plate.

He made himself as small as possible, hoping that the driver of the sedan wouldn't be able to see his hiding spot in front of a large four-wheel-drive truck, the sides caked with mud.

Paige hadn't imagined it. Somehow, the gunmen had pinpointed their location. The fact that Mike had obtained a rental car under a fake name was likely the main reason they hadn't been discovered already.

Should they stay? Or go? The headlights grew brighter as the sedan rolled behind their SUV.

The booster seat!

Miles held his breath and prayed the occupants in the car wouldn't see it.

Guide me, Lord. Help me keep Paige and Abby safe from harm.

The car rolled past their rented SUV to the next car, yet Miles didn't move, willing the driver to keep going. When the vehicle went around the building, he leaped to his feet and quickly entered the motel room.

"We need to get out of here, right now. Before they come back around," he said urgently.

Thankfully, Paige didn't argue. She crossed over to where Abby was sleeping. "Do I have time to pack our things?"

"No." He quickly stashed Jason's papers back in the padded envelope and tucked them in the inside pocket of his jacket.

"Abby? We're going for a ride," Paige said, lifting her daughter into her arms. The little girl didn't answer and Miles found he was glad about that. He didn't want her to be frightened again.

And he was getting sick and tired of these gunmen tracking him down.

Miles pulled his phone out of his pocket and crushed it beneath the heel of his boot. "Give me your phone, too. I don't want to take any chances."

Paige nodded and watched as he stomped on her phone as well. She grabbed both her winter coat and Abby's. "That's fine, but we can't take anything else. I'm sorry."

"It's okay. She has her elephant. That's what really matters."

He crossed to the door and opened it a crack. "We're the third stall down. See the way I'm backed into the spot? Let's go."

Paige nodded and darted outside, heading toward the car. He was right behind her, keeping a sharp eye out for any sign of the sedan.

He stowed the computer on the floor of the passenger seat as Paige wrestled Abby into the booster.

"Get inside," he bit out. "Worry about buckling her in later."

Paige did as he asked, moving all the way inside the backseat so he could shut the door behind her. He swiftly slid behind the wheel then started the car, wincing as the sound of the engine seemed ridiculously loud.

Without turning on the headlights, he drove around the building, taking the same path that the sedan had traversed, his logic being that if they were going to circle around again, he could get out onto the highway without being seen.

At least, that was the plan.

When he reached the farthest side of the building, he slowed to a crawl, easing the nose of his car around the corner, hoping that the sedan wasn't still sitting there, waiting.

The coast was clear.

Breathing a sigh of relief, he headed straight for the highway.

Just when he was ready to flip on the headlights, he saw the sedan coming around the corner of the building. They must have realized one of the parked cars was gone.

He hit the gas, anxious to get as far away as possible, but when he looked in his rearview mirror, the sedan was coming up behind him.

"Stay down, both of you," he ordered, as he hammered the gas pedal to the floor.

He could hear Paige scrambling to pull Abby out of the booster seat and down onto the floor between the seats. He could hear Paige praying out loud in an attempt to reassure her daughter.

The highway stretched before him, no other vehicles in sight, which was good since he was driving way over the speed limit. But it was bad, too, because it made losing the sedan that much more difficult.

A loud blast of gunfire made him flinch. The sedan was still behind him, not gaining ground, but not dropping back, either.

He gritted his teeth and focused on keeping the SUV on the road, wondering how much time they had before one of the bullets hit its mark.

NINE

On the floor of the backseat, Paige huddled over Abby, praying as the sound of gunfire echoed through the darkness. Just when they'd thought they were safe, the gunmen had found them again.

"Hang on. It's going to get bumpy," Miles said in a grim tone.

She didn't like not being able to see what was going on. She felt a burst of speed, and the vehicle jerked, as if he'd abruptly changed lanes. Paige did her best to use the winter coats she'd brought as a cushion around Abby, protecting her daughter at all costs.

Another gunshot echoed through the night, and Paige found herself holding her breath, hoping and praying they hadn't been hit.

The SUV bounced wildly, sending her flying sideways against the back of the driver's seat. The constant jostling movements continued, making it difficult for her to stay in one place. The coats helped keep Abby secure, which she was thankful for. Paige planted her hand against the driver's seat and the backseat cushion in an attempt to stay over Abby, wondering what in the world Miles was doing. It felt as if they were driving over rocks.

Then it occurred to her that he might be going off the road on purpose, knowing the sedan might not be able to follow.

Sure enough, glancing up through the windows she could see tree branches, bare of any leaves, looming overhead, as if they were driving into the woods. Logically, that didn't seem possible, but she couldn't see anything else to tell her where they were.

The gunfire seemed to have stopped, the interior of the car silent except for Abby's whimpering. She reached out to stroke her daughter, wishing she knew for sure if the sedan was still behind them.

Nevertheless, she trusted the handsome detective enough to know he would tell her once the danger was over. The SUV continued to bounce crazily from side to side, convincing her they weren't safe yet.

Dear Lord, please protect us from harm. Guide Miles to safety!

Paige had no idea how long she was crouched on the floor of the SUV comforting Abby the best she could, but it seemed like forever. Her knees were becoming sore, but she ignored the discomfort, trying to stay focused on the fact that the gunfire had stopped.

After another few minutes, Miles broke the silence. "We've lost them for now. You can get up off the floor."

Cautiously, she poked her head up to peer at their surroundings. There were trees on either side of the vehicle. "Where are we?"

"No clue," Miles said in a somber tone. "And we're going to have to walk soon."

"Walk?" The idea of carrying Abby over the rough terrain didn't sound at all appealing. She already felt exhausted and they hadn't walked a single step. Not to mention, it was freezing outside. Even with their winter coats, Abby would be cold. "Why?"

"Because I'm fairly certain they have the license plate number of our car. I'm not willing to risk your life or Abby's. We need to lose them once and for all."

She swallowed around the dryness in her throat, meeting Miles's gaze in the rearview mirror. "But it's too cold for a little girl," she protested weakly.

"We'll keep her warm." The absolute confidence in his tone was reassuring. "Don't worry, we'll find a way out of this."

Ironically, despite everything that had happened since the night they'd first met, she believed him.

Miles would safeguard them, no matter what. Risking his own life, if needed.

Miles inwardly seethed at how terribly he'd failed Paige and Abby, two innocent lives completely dependent upon him for protection.

Leaving the phones behind and abandoning the SUV were the only things he could think of that would keep them out of the line of fire. Although they'd tried that before, yet they'd still been found. He'd get in touch with one of his siblings eventually, but not until they'd found a way to get out of the area.

Although how he'd manage that, he had no idea.

A moment of panic hit hard.

Miles pulled himself together with concentrated effort. He could do this. What he needed to focus on was taking things one step at a time.

Looking at the thick brush up ahead gave him an idea. He could hide the SUV there, and the twigs covering the ground would help camouflage their tracks as they took off on foot.

He drove into the brush, wincing as the brambles scraped against the paint. Shutting off the engine, he turned in his seat. "We'll head out the back when you're ready."

"Okay." Paige was putting Abby's coat, hat and mittens on over her footy pajamas. The pink elephant was looking a little worse for wear, but he was glad Abby still had it. He wished the little girl had boots, but he could always carry her close to his body, beneath his coat.

If she'd let him.

He hit the button that would unlatch the back door, allowing it to spring upright. Then he crawled between the seats, joining Paige and Abby in the back. He double checked to make sure that he still had the papers Jason had sent to him.

"We're going on a little adventure, Abby, you up for that?" he asked while Paige was pulling her coat on.

Abby nodded and Paige smiled encouragingly. "We're ready, right, sweetie?"

"I'll go first." There wasn't a lot of space, but he managed to get up and over the backseat into the spacious area beyond. The air outside was cold, and he emitted puffs of steam with every exhale. He glanced around to make sure they were alone before he gestured for Paige and Abby to follow.

Paige lifted Abby up over the seat first, and he was relieved to find that the little girl seemed to have no qualms about going into his arms. He opened his coat and brought her in close to his chest, making sure the elephant was firmly planted between him and Abby, before zipping the lower part of his jacket for added warmth. When he had Abby and Ellie secured against him, he reached out a hand to assist Paige.

When they were out of the vehicle, they stepped back out of the way so he could bring the door down.

"Which way?" Paige asked in a whisper, looking around in confusion.

Miles took a moment to get his bearings. "I believe there's a small town to the south. Follow me."

He stepped forward, but Paige grabbed his arm. "I can carry her," she said.

"She'll be warmer this way. Come on. We have to hurry."

Paige nodded and fell into step behind him. He led the way through the thickest portion of the brush in an effort to cover their tracks. Even once they cleared the trees, he made sure to place his feet in areas that wouldn't leave prints behind. The frozen earth worked in their favor and he was glad the snow flurries hadn't amounted to much in the way of accumulation.

Paige didn't say anything, and of course neither did Abby. The little girl rested against him, her body radiating heat, and he wondered if he should let Paige carry her for a while, if for no other reason than to warm up.

Yet he wanted to make good time, to make sure they could get far enough away from the spot they'd left the car, in case the gunmen had decided to follow them on foot. He was fairly sure the SUV had made a path that a blind man could follow.

Peering through the darkness, Miles thought he could see lights from the town up ahead. They were nothing more than tiny pinpricks of light, but he resolutely made his way in that direction.

There was a larger town nearby and to the north, and he was hoping the gunmen would assume they'd head in that direction. Truthfully, it had been a toss-up as to which way was better. A larger town would be easier to hide in, but he was banking on the fact that people residing in a small town might be friendlier, willing to help out a couple with a small child.

All he needed was a phone to call Mitch or Mike. A vehicle would be great, but he was hoping one of his brothers could at least pick them up and take them someplace safe.

Paige's breathing grew more labored and he slowed his pace so she wouldn't have to work so hard to keep up. As they walked, he found himself praying again.

Keep us safe. Don't let these men find us.

It occurred to Miles that he'd prayed more since meeting Paige than he had in the years since Dawn died. And even as the words echoed over and over in his mind like a mantra, he knew that his prayers were focused mostly on Paige and Abby.

They deserved to be safe from harm. Surely that was part of God's plan, wasn't it?

"I need a break," Paige said between gasping breaths.

He stopped and turned toward her with concern. "Are you all right?"

She leaned over, bracing her hands on her thighs, and coughed several times into her coat, as if attempting to muffle the sound. "Sorry," she murmured. "The cold air makes my asthma flare up."

"Do you have an inhaler?"

She shook her head. "Back at the motel, but not with me."

"I wish you would have said something earlier," Miles said, wondering if the town had a pharmacy. But then he realized that wouldn't be smart, if the people tracking them were able to hack into computers, then he couldn't afford to leave an electronic trail.

"I'm sorry, I didn't want to slow us down."

He felt bad for bringing it up. "No problem, I just want to be sure you're okay."

"I'll manage."

He knew she would and they had plenty of other things to worry about. Such as being out here in the open. Granted he was doing his best to use the coverage offered by scattered trees, but overall, the field they were crossing now didn't have much in the way of protection.

After several long moments, Paige straightened. Even in the darkness, her skin looked pale.

"Okay, I'm ready."

He refrained from pointing out that she didn't look ready. Her coughing had stopped, so he nodded and gestured with his hand. "See the lights in the distance?" he asked.

She nodded.

"That's our destination. I'll walk slower, and if you need another break, don't hesitate to let me know."

"I'll be fine. The sooner we get to the town, the safer we'll be."

No argument there. He turned and resumed walking, making a conscious effort to shorten his stride. It wasn't easy; the need to hurry nagged at him. And based on Paige's asthma, he decided against allowing her to carry Abby.

"Miles?"

He stopped again, turning to glance at her. Did she need another break already? "Yes?"

"What is—the plan—once we get—to town?" The gasping pauses in her voice worried him.

"Convince someone to let us borrow a phone," he said. "Don't worry. One of my brothers will help us. For right now, let's just keep moving, okay?"

She nodded without saying anything more and he was glad, hoping she'd conserve her energy for the trek ahead of them. He angled toward an old bale of hay that was located about a hundred yards away. If they could reach it, they could rest again for a few more minutes.

The lights hadn't gotten much brighter, forcing him to acknowledge they were still several miles away from civilization.

For the first time, he considered the possibility that they might not arrive in town before the sun came up, the way he'd originally planned. Moving in the relative safety that the darkness provided was one thing.

Walking in daylight would be far more difficult. The trees and shrubs wouldn't offer enough protection from anyone driving past.

Yet pushing Paige to go faster wasn't an option, either.

He had to hope and pray they'd make it in time.

Paige drew the front of her coat up to cover her mouth and nose, hoping to blunt the hard pinch of the cold air in her lungs.

She absolutely hated feeling like a wimp. Miles was carrying Abby, yet she still found it difficult to keep up. Her legs were strong enough, but inhaling the cold air was like breathing shards of glass, sharp edges rasping along her throat.

Breathing through the fabric of her jacket seemed to help a bit, and she kept her head down, fighting the urge to cough.

Glancing up, she battled a wave of despair that the lights from the town were still so far away. It seemed like they'd already been walking forever, but she knew it was probably closer to ninety minutes.

Focused on putting one foot in front of the other, following in Miles's footsteps as closely as possible, she didn't realize he'd stopped before she bumped into him.

"What's wrong?" she asked in a harsh whisper.

"Nothing is wrong. It's time for another break." He leaned against the tall, round bale of hay that she just now noticed.

"I'm doing okay," she protested in a muffled tone.

"A few minutes rest will do us both good," he said firmly. "And staying here against the hay, we're hidden from view."

"You really think they're out there, searching for us?"

"Yes." The single word hit her with tsunami

force and she literally backed up a step. "I'm sorry, Paige, but you deserve the truth. I'm afraid they're not going to stop searching for us."

She forced herself to nod, then gathered her strength and went to stand beside him, leaning against the hay. It was only once she began to shiver that he pushed away.

"Let's go."

The field stretched endlessly ahead of them but over time the lights actually grew brighter. The buildings grew larger in size, too.

A sense of relief washed over her when she could actually read the lighted sign over a gas station. Paige found herself walking faster, anxious to get there as soon as possible.

The faint light of dawn was edging over the horizon by the time they reached the gas station. The place was closed, but Paige didn't care.

Being in a town meant seeing people. Hopefully people who would help them.

"Now what?" she asked, as they rested against the wall of the gas station. The fabric over her mouth had eased the urge to cough, for which she was grateful.

Miles peered at his watch. "It's five minutes past five now. The sign on the front of the station's convenience store says they open at five thirty. We'll get something to eat, use the restrooms and then figure out where to go from there.

Hopefully the gas station attendant will let us use the phone."

She nodded, liking that plan. Less than thirty minutes wasn't too long.

A car drove past, startling her badly. Miles had chosen the side of the building farthest from the road as the best place for them to wait, but she still held her breath, relaxing only when she could tell the car was a light beige in color.

The minutes ticked by with infinite slowness, but at five twenty a rusty car pulled up, and a skinny young man climbed out and unlocked the gas station door.

They remained hidden alongside the building until the guy hit the lights, illuminating the entire gas station, including the pumps.

"Let's go." Miles eased away from the building and walked over to enter the gas station, holding the door open for her.

The interior was blessedly warm and it was all Paige could do to stay upright. The attendant looked at them in surprise, as if he hadn't expected to have early morning visitors.

"Check out what you'd like to eat," Miles said, loud enough for the guy to hear. "The muffins look good to me."

"Me, too," she agreed. The coolers were full of drinks, including chocolate milk for Abby, so she crossed over to grab a carton, bringing it back to the counter.

"The coffee should be ready soon," the gas station employee offered.

"That would be great," she said with a smile. "Thanks."

There were small tables off to one side of the store, unfortunately right near the large windows. Paige told herself it was better to be able to see who was coming, even though she'd rather have stayed hidden. She took several breaths of warm air, feeling the tightness easing from her throat.

"Abby, do you need to use the bathroom?" Paige asked, as her daughter lifted a sleepy head from Miles's shoulder.

The little girl nodded, so Paige took her hand and walked with her to the bathroom. They took turns, then washed up, before heading back to where Miles waited.

He had already eaten his muffin and rose to his feet. "I'll be right back."

She expected him to head to the restrooms, but instead he walked back up to the counter. She heard him speaking to the skinny man, who reluctantly handed over his phone.

She said a brief prayer, then she and Abby ate their muffins, too. Ten minutes later, Miles had made his call and returned from the bathroom.

He purchased two cups of coffee and left a nice tip for the attendant.

"Mike will be here soon," he told her. "Get something else, too, if you're still hungry."

"Abby? Do you want something more to eat?"

The little girl shook her head, too busy playing with Ellie. She was making the elephant walk along the edge of the table, bobbing her head from side to side as if they were having a silent conversation.

Paige sighed, wishing the little girl would find her voice. But after being under what seemed like constant fire from determined gunmen, she was too afraid to push.

"I still don't understand how they found us," she said in a low voice, hoping Abby wasn't paying attention.

"I don't either," Miles admitted gruffly. "I made a couple of phone calls to my boss and to the precinct, but I find it hard to believe my crusty old captain would do something like this."

She looked up at Miles, her eyes widening in horror. "I called Ralph. Do you think it's possible that my call was traced?"

Miles didn't say anything and she covered her mouth with her hand to keep from crying. What if this was her fault? All because she didn't listen when Miles told her not to call anyone?

"Don't," he ground out, apparently reading the

expression on her face. He pulled her into a quick hug. "We don't know that Ralph is responsible, either. Focus on the fact that we're safe and we're going to stay that way."

She made a silent promise to listen to Miles from now on, no matter what.

Twenty minutes later, Miles rose to his feet. "Mike is here, see the black car? Let's go."

She lifted Abby into her arms, and this time Miles let her carry Abby. She slid into the backseat, leaving Miles to sit up front with his brother. Mike was wearing a black hat pulled low on his forehead and shiny, reflective sunglasses. The sun was slowly rising, so she didn't think they looked out of place.

They'd barely gotten settled when Mike said in a low, urgent tone, "Get down. All of you. Hurry!"

Paige dropped down, taking Abby with her, wondering if this was a nightmare. What happened? They should be safe!

Mike cruised up to a pump and shut off the engine. He climbed out of the car, and began fiddling with the gas tank. It seemed to take forever for him to get the gas cap off and place the nozzle in the tank.

In the space between the seats she could see Miles was doing his best to cram his six-foot frame beneath the dashboard.

"What did Mike see?" she whispered.

Miles stared at her for a long moment. "Black car with tinted windows rolling past the gas station."

She sucked in a harsh breath. The gunmen had once again caught up with them.

TEN

The desperate fear in Paige's eyes wrenched at his heart. He wanted to reassure her they were safe, but that wasn't exactly true. Miles couldn't believe the dark sedan had shown up. It was almost as if they had known exactly what he'd been thinking.

Pulling his large frame into a ball as small as possible wasn't easy. If anyone came close enough to look inside, they'd find him without a problem. From where he was hunched down on the floor of the passenger seat, he could see Mike was filling the gas tank, as if he didn't have a care in the world. When his brother finished, he replaced the nozzle in the pump, replaced the gas cap, then turned and walked inside the convenience store.

At first, Miles was stunned that Mike had left them inside the car. Then he realized Mike couldn't pay for gas with a credit card.

Still, Miles didn't like being vulnerable. From his position on the floor, he couldn't see the black sedan. What if the occupants came over and opened fire? They'd be dead before he could blink.

His gun felt useless in his hand. Miles considered whether or not to risk lifting his head to see if the black sedan with the tinted windows was still out there. The seconds ticked by endlessly. When he thought he couldn't stand not knowing a second longer, he caught a glimpse of his brother approaching the car, head down as he jingled his keys.

Mike lifted his head, opened the driver's side door and slid in behind the wheel. He didn't look toward Miles or say anything at all, simply started the car and drove away.

Five minutes later, his brother gestured with his hand. "Everyone can get up now, we're clear."

"Where's the black sedan?" Miles asked. Unfolding himself wasn't easy. His muscles were stiff and cramped. He could see that Paige was getting Abby settled in the backseat.

"They drove by twice, moving with exaggerated slowness, which is why I made sure to act as if I was alone," his brother explained. "I didn't want anything to tip them off."

Miles finally managed to twist around so he was in the seat. "Thanks, Mike."

"You have some seriously determined people after you, bro," Mike said, his gaze serious. "You've escaped from them three times now."

"Technically four," Miles corrected wryly. "If you count the attack near the post office."

Mike didn't smile. "Are you any closer to nailing the guy behind all this?" he asked.

"Not as close as I'd like," Miles admitted, scrubbing his hands over his face. "And I'm sorry about the rental car. I left it back in the brush. It's dinged up a bit."

"Forget about it. I paid for the maximum insurance. Oh, and just so you know, this car is registered to Roberta Parker."

"Who's that?"

"A friend of a friend. No direct connection with the Callahan name." Mike frowned. "Although the SUV was also registered to a person that couldn't be linked to the Callahans either."

"The fake ID worked like a charm," Miles hastened to reassure him. "They couldn't ID us from the vehicle, but somehow they figured out our location. I thought the fact that the SUV was a rental might tip them off, so we decided to try to sneak away."

For all the good it had done.

Mike grimaced. "Yeah, I thought about the rental car aspect, too. This vehicle is solid, Roberta lives in Greenland, which is just outside of Milwaukee. Shouldn't trigger any red flags."

"Thanks again," Miles said, lightly punching his younger brother in the arm. He glanced at the direction Mike was driving. "Where are you taking us?"

"To Roberta Parker's house."

"Huh?" Miles thought he couldn't have heard that right. "I don't understand."

"You can't keep running from one motel to the next." Mike's tone was reasonable. "This friend of a friend happened to be house sitting for Roberta Parker so we're going to borrow the house and the car." His brother slanted him a sideways look. "It would be nice if you could manage to leave this place exactly the way you found it. Same for the car."

Miles grimaced and nodded. "I promise to do my best."

His brother sighed. "Guess I can't ask for more than that."

"A house sounds wonderful." Paige spoke up from the backseat. "Thank you, Michael."

His brother's mouth quirked up in a crooked smile. "You're welcome, Paige."

A flash of jealousy caught Miles off guard. He tried to hide his reaction, knowing that Paige was just being nice, but he couldn't seem to erase the scowl from his features.

"There's a laptop computer in the house. I checked before borrowing the car," Mike went on, oblivious to his older brother's inner turmoil. "There's even a landline hooked up to a fax machine, so you have everything you need to continue working the case."

Despite his annoyance, Miles couldn't help being impressed. "You outdid yourself this time, Mikey."

His brother's eyes narrowed at the childhood nickname. "A simple thank-you is enough."

A good fifteen minutes later, Mike turned into a quiet neighborhood and pulled up in front of a brown house with yellow trim. Roberta Parker's house was modest, but so much better than any of the motels they'd stayed in, that Miles knew it would be like living in luxury. For one thing, they could cook their own food, so they wouldn't have to risk going out. The best part was that the house and the car were both in the name of the same person. No way would any of the computer gurus from Sci-Tech find them here.

Mike parked in the two-car garage that was connected to the house. They waited until the garage door closed before getting out of the vehicle.

"Come on, sweetie," Paige encouraged as her daughter blinked up at her sleepily. "You can rest some more once we're inside, okay?"

Abby yawned, nodded and rubbed at her eyes. But she still didn't speak.

"Sure is a quiet little kid," Mike said as he unlocked the door.

Miles exchanged a glance with Paige, and the sadness in her eyes hit hard.

"She didn't used to be," Paige said in a low tone, before brushing past them to carry Abby inside.

"The bedrooms are down the hall to the right," Mike pointed out. "Paige and Abby might want to take the master, since the spare bedroom only has a twin."

"Good idea," Miles agreed. His feet would hang off the end of the twin bed, but that didn't matter as he wasn't planning to do much sleeping anyway.

He needed to step up his investigative efforts in a big way. So far, they'd done more running than anything constructive. They were safe in the Parker home, but the way things had been going, he couldn't afford to waste any more time.

"If you need anything, call," Mike said.

"Wait, don't leave yet. We'll need some groceries, food for Abby at the very least." Miles started a list, and when Paige joined them a few minutes later, apparently leaving Abby in the bedroom, he gestured to it. "Add whatever you think we may need to cover us for a couple of days."

"Sure." Paige opened the fridge, then quickly jotted down what she needed.

"I'll be right back," Mike said as he slipped the list into his pocket.

Once Miles and Paige were alone in the house, there was a moment of awkward silence. He tried to think of something to say, but his normal easy way with women seemed to have abandoned him. Maybe because he cared about Paige more than he should.

"I expect Abby will be up soon, so I'm happy to make breakfast once your brother returns with the groceries," she offered.

"Thanks. That will give me time to begin digging into the case," he said, gesturing at the laptop computer that was sitting on the counter.

She tipped her head to the side, her expression curious. "What are you going to search for?"

Good question. He reached inside his jacket and removed the papers Jason had sent him. "I'm going to start with the information in here. A lot of it is over my head, and I really need to figure out why Jason sent this to me. There must be something important in here. Otherwise, why bother?"

Paige nodded slowly. She looked as if she might ask another question, but Abby padded into the kitchen, carrying Ellie under one arm and sucking her thumb.

"Are you hungry?" Paige asked her daughter.

Abby nodded.

"Mike will be back soon with groceries so I'll make your favorite breakfast, okay?"

Abby nodded again, without removing the thumb from her mouth.

Miles watched the little girl climb up on the sofa and curl up in the corner, resting her cheek on the stuffed elephant's head. His gaze clashed with Paige's, sharing an unspoken concern about Abby's welfare.

He wished he knew exactly what she'd seen on the ChatTime link that night. The way these gunmen kept coming after them, he knew that the child must have seen something significant.

But what, exactly?

He didn't know. All he could do was to pray that Abby would soon feel safe enough to talk to them.

Cooking soothed Paige's nerves. She had to admit that staying in a house was so much nicer than being in a musty motel room.

The muffins they'd consumed at the convenience store weren't enough to hold them over until lunchtime. Abby loved French toast, so that's what Paige was making.

Her eyes burned with exhaustion. She hadn't slept through the night since this nightmare began, but maybe tonight, if they were truly safe, she'd be able to get some rest.

Miles needed sleep, too. He looked rougher around the edges than she felt.

Scary how much she'd come to depend on him and his family. Michael was a nice guy, but Miles was the one she couldn't stop staring at.

Couldn't stop thinking about.

Couldn't stop longing for.

She jerked herself from those dangerous thoughts, knowing that it was ridiculous to daydream about a man like Miles Callahan. A man that good-looking could have any woman he wanted. Besides, she trusted him to keep them safe, but anything more? Not happening.

She flipped the slices of egg-battered bread, adding a pat of butter to the top of each one. She poured chocolate milk into a cup for Abby and set that on the table next to where Miles was working.

"Breakfast is ready," she called out.

Abby slid off the couch and came over, dragging her stuffed elephant with her.

"Let's not get Ellie all sticky, okay?" Paige took the elephant and set her on the seat of an empty chair, then brought in a large platter of French toast and a bottle of maple syrup she'd found in the fridge.

Miles closed the laptop and pushed it aside. He smiled at Paige and Abby. "Looks great. Shall we pray?"

Paige shouldn't have been surprised by the way

he'd taken the lead on the pre-meal prayer, but she was. She took her seat and then waited for Abby to bow her head before doing the same.

"Dear Lord, we thank You for providing us a wonderful place to stay and for the food we are about to eat. We also thank You for keeping us safe in Your care. Amen."

"Amen," Paige echoed.

Abby lifted her head without speaking, but she smiled when Paige put two slices of French toast on her plate and began cutting them into small pieces. "Miles, I'm really glad you're praying."

He hesitated, his fork halfway to his mouth. "It's been a long time for me," he said. He chewed and swallowed, then added, "We were raised to believe in God and the whole family still attends church services on Sunday followed by brunch at my mom's house. Since my dad died, it's just my mom and Nan living there now, but we make an effort to see them each week."

She was touched by the idea of Miles and his tough looking brothers visiting their mother and grandmother each week. "Sounds lovely. I'm sure your mom and grandmother appreciate seeing you all together."

"They do. But we appreciate them just as much." Miles took another bite of his food, regarding her thoughtfully. "They'd like you."

She stared at him for a moment, then tore her gaze away. "Tell me about your family."

"My dad was once the Milwaukee chief of police," he said. "He was killed in the line of duty about nine months ago."

"I'm sorry for your loss," she said softly.

"Thanks. As far as the rest of my family goes, you already met Mike and Mitch. Michael is a private investigator and the only one in the family who doesn't have a career serving the community. My dad was not very happy with his career choice, and I think his attitude really bothered Mike a lot, although he never says anything about it."

She nodded, understanding how difficult it must have been for Mike to go against his father's wishes. "You mentioned Mitch is an arson investigator. I assume he was a firefighter at one point, too, right?"

Miles nodded. "Our oldest brother, Marc works for the FBI. Matthew and Maddy are the twins, Maddy is the youngest one by three minutes, something Matthew never lets her forget. Matthew is a new canine cop, Duke is his K9 partner and Maddy is a lawyer working for the DA's office."

Paige felt as if her career in accounting was dull and boring in comparison. Although after everything that she'd been through, she couldn't deny that dull and boring sounded pretty good right now.

"And you're a homicide detective. Very impressive."

Mitch's expression hardened and he stabbed a piece of French toast with more force than was necessary. "Not a very good one, since I can't seem to figure out who keeps trying to kill us."

"You've kept us safe since the very first night you arrived at my house," she corrected him. "I know there's no way I could have faced any of this alone."

His blue eyes meshed with her green ones and the warmth radiating from him made it impossible for her to breathe normally. She tore her gaze away, fearing he'd see too much.

She needed to get a grip on her wayward emotions.

"How is your breakfast, Abby?" she asked, focusing on her daughter. The only person who truly needed her attention.

The little girl smiled and bobbed her head up and down. Paige finished her meal, pushed her plate away and rose to her feet. After carrying the dirty dishes to the sink, she brought back a damp washcloth and began wiping away the sticky syrup smudges from Abby's face and hands.

"Ready to watch a movie?" Abby had watched more television in the past few days than she had in an entire month, but there wasn't much Paige could do about it. They'd been forced to leave the books and toys behind.

Once she found a kids' channel for Abby, Paige turned and walked back to the kitchen. Miles was standing there, rinsing their dishes.

"I'd like to try talking to Abby again," he said in a low voice. "See if she'll say anything more about what she witnessed that night."

"I don't think that's a good idea," Paige protested. "She needs time to recuperate, time to feel safe."

"I know. But so far, I'm having trouble deciphering Jason's notes. I need something more to go on."

It was heart-wrenching to realize that the outcome of his investigation depended upon what a five-year-old child witnessed. Paige knew he was right, but concern for her daughter overrode everything else.

"We'll see how the day goes," she hedged. "She hasn't started talking yet, anyway, so I'm not sure how much help she'll be."

"Even answering yes-or-no questions is a place to start," Miles said encouragingly. He glanced over to where Abby was sitting on the sofa again, her thumb having found its way back into her mouth. "I don't want to upset her, either." He turned back toward Paige and he was close enough that she could breathe in his clean, musky scent. "And you have to admit that having the truth come out might make her feel better."

Paige remembered how Abby had seemed to want Miles to understand what had happened. How her daughter had gazed at him, let him hold her and carry her.

As much as she hated to admit it, her daughter trusted Miles, probably more than Paige did.

"Maybe." She gestured to the dishes. "I'll take care of these."

Miles shook his head. "My mom and Nan would have my head if I so much as hinted that doing dishes was women's work."

That made her smile. "You're right. I think I'd like your mom and your grandmother just fine."

"I'll wash, you dry." Miles ran hot water into one side of the sink. "I'd appreciate you looking through Jason's notes, too. Maybe with your experience there, you'll catch something I missed."

Doubtful, but Paige agreed since there wasn't anything else to do. Doing dishes with Miles created an intimacy she didn't understand. It wasn't as if she hadn't shared living space with a man before.

Although, if she was being honest, she'd admit that Travis had rarely felt the need to chip in and help with daily chores. He'd claimed he needed to work, but she soon realized that was just his excuse to leave to meet up with one of his numerous lady friends.

She reminded herself that no matter what Travis had done, he hadn't deserved to be murdered. And she still needed to find a way to tell Abby her father was in God's hands now.

Miles cleaned up the counter, then went back over to the table where he'd left the computer and Jason's notes. When she finished putting the last of the dishes away, she joined him.

"Here, we'll split them down the middle," Miles suggested. "See if anything jumps out at you."

"Okay." She took a deep breath, cleared her mind the way she did before starting any large project and began to read. At first she was completely lost, but the science behind the robotics eventually drew her interest.

If what she was reading was true, Sci-Tech was very close to creating technology that would allow people with spinal cord injuries to walk again. Electrodes strategically placed along both sides of the spine could recreate nerve function. Programming the electrical impulses could fire the nerves to enable walking.

Revolutionizing the artificial intelligence industry.

The phone rang, startling her so badly that she dropped the papers she'd been reading.

Miles rose to his feet with a frown and crossed over to the landline. "Hello?"

Paige held her breath, watching the big, handsome detective, fearing the worst. But when his expression cleared, she let out a heavy sigh.

"Wait a minute. Back up, Mike. What do you mean, *followed*?" Miles looked over at Paige, his brow furrowed as he listened to his brother.

"Dark red jeep? I can't say that I remember seeing it, but let me check with Paige."

"No," she said, shaking her head. "I haven't seen one."

"When did you see it?" Miles demanded, returning to the phone conversation. "Is this place compromised?"

There was a pause, then Miles nodded. "Good. Okay, then…listen, you need to be careful. Maybe you should take the entire family on a vacation to keep them safe."

Paige shivered, hating the thought that the entire Callahan family might be in danger because Miles had agreed to help her.

And if anything happened to his family, it would be all her fault.

ELEVEN

"Yeah, right," Mike said with a snort. "You must be crazy if you think I could manage to pull that off. Maybe I could come up with a way to get Mom and Nan out of the house, but the entire family? Dream on."

Miles gripped the receiver so tightly he feared it might crack. "You have to do this for me, Mike. I need to know that the family is safe. The fact that you picked up the tail proves they know who you are and where you live. Which means they know where Mom and Nan live, too. And now that Dad's gone..." He didn't have to finish.

There was a brief silence as Mike considered his options. "I'll talk to the guys. I'm pretty sure I can convince them that we need to take turns staying at Mom's house. Although, you know, Mom is going to ask questions about why we're suddenly spending the night. What do you want me to tell her?"

Miles didn't want to lie to his mother and

grandmother, but he also didn't want them to know the entire truth, either. They both worried about the six of them enough; he didn't want to add to their burden. "Tell her that I'm investigating a homicide and that you, Mitch and Matthew are going to take turns staying over. I don't want her to know any details, understand?"

"Yeah, yeah." Mike sounded grumpy. "Anything else?"

"Not right now, but thanks." Miles cleared his throat. "Stay safe, Mike. I'll call you if I need you."

"Back at you." His brother hung up.

Miles replaced the receiver and stared blindly down at the phone. He wasn't at all happy that his brother had been followed. And why on earth would someone use a dark red Jeep to tail someone in the first place? Most crooks tried to blend in by using nondescript cars, not ostentatious ones.

He pressed his fingers to his temples in an attempt to ease the throbbing. The lack of sleep was wearing on him. Nothing about this case made sense.

Because he was missing something. A link that would tie everything together.

If only he could find it.

Turning away from the phone, he glanced at Abby curled in the corner of the sofa, sucking her thumb. Her wide gaze was locked on the cartoon movie she was watching and he knew he couldn't afford to waste any more time.

He needed to talk to Paige's daughter about what had frightened her so badly the night she'd dropped the tablet.

Now. Before anyone else was harmed.

He took a step toward Abby, but something in his expression must have tipped Paige off to his intent, because she jumped up from her seat and planted herself firmly in his path.

"What are you doing?" Her voice was soft yet fierce, a momma bear protecting her baby.

He searched her green-gold gaze. "You know I have to talk to her, Paige."

"We agreed to wait."

"No, we agreed to see how the day progressed," he corrected, holding on to his temper by a thread. He understood her concern, but she had to know by now that he had Abby's best interests at heart. "And now my family is in danger, too. We're running out of time."

Her eyes beseeched him not to do anything to upset her daughter, making him feel lower than a snake slithering along in the grass. "Please don't do this," she whispered.

"I have to try."

She crossed her arms over her chest, staring him down, but he didn't budge. Hardening his heart, he brushed past her toward the sofa. As he approached, he could see the cartoon show had just ended, so he scooped up the remote and quickly shut off the television.

Abby looked at him with a pout. She gestured toward the television, wordlessly indicating she wanted it turned back on.

He sat beside her on the sofa, leaving a bit of space between them so she wouldn't feel crowded. "Sweetheart, I need to ask you a few questions before I turn the television back on, okay?"

Abby shook her head and tried to reach past him for the remote.

"No, Abby. Questions first, then television." Gently but firmly, Miles eased the little girl back into her spot on the sofa.

Abby sulked, but her mood didn't last long. She picked up her elephant and tipped her head to the side, looking up at him, obviously waiting for him to start.

Paige came over and perched on the edge of the sofa next to her daughter, obviously intending to intervene if things didn't go well. He swallowed a flash of annoyance. He'd never hurt a child in his life, and didn't plan to start now. But he couldn't deny that his questions might cause the little girl to become distressed, so he forced himself to relax his features and kept his gaze soft.

"Abby, we need to find out what happened to your daddy."

The little girl frowned and pulled the elephant closer. Her thumb slipped back into her mouth and she was so adorable, his heart squeezed painfully in his chest.

"I'm going to ask you some questions about the night you saw your daddy on the ChatTime link, okay?"

Abby's wide gaze clung to his and he expected her to shake her head, but she surprised him by nodding in agreement.

Encouraged, he smiled. "Good girl. So…did your daddy talk to you that night you got scared and hid under the bed?"

Abby gave a jerky nod.

"When he first called, did he want to talk to you? Or to your mom?"

Abby reached up and patted her mom's arm. Paige looked surprised by the news.

Miles lifted a brow, glancing at Paige. "Did Travis often talk to you via the link, too?" he asked Paige.

"No. The ChatTime link was mostly for Abby."

He wondered why Travis had changed his routine that night. "Your phone was in the kitchen, right?"

"Yes." Paige frowned. "Why?"

"Was it turned on? With a full battery?"

Her brow furrowed. "I think so, but to be honest, the ringer was probably off. I was getting calls by mistake in the middle of the night, so I powered it off. I'm not sure I remembered to turn it back on."

So it was possible that Travis had tried to call Paige, and when she hadn't picked up, he'd used the ChatTime link to connect with his daughter. Imagining how the scenario might have played out made him feel better.

"Okay, Abby, your dad used the ChatTime link because he wanted to talk to your mom. Is that right?"

The little girl nodded again.

Here's where things got a little dicey. Miles knew he had to tread carefully, because if he upset Abby too much, Paige would intervene, abruptly ending the conversation. "Did something happen before you could bring the tablet over to your mom?" he asked gently.

Abby's eyes clung to his, reflecting her inner turmoil as she nodded again.

"It's okay, honey," Paige said, reaching out to smooth Abby's hair away from her forehead. "No one can hurt you. We're safe here."

"Your mom is right, Abby," he said in a calm, soothing voice. "I will protect you and your mom no matter what. Okay?" The child nodded again, edging closer to her mother's side.

He tried to think of the best way to broach his next few questions. "Did you see anyone on the screen besides your daddy?"

Abby nodded, then turned and hid her face against her mother as if she didn't want to think about what she'd witnessed.

"I'm here, Abby," Paige whispered, bending over to gather her daughter into her arms. "I love you."

Miles watched Paige cuddle the little girl, his heart wrenching in his chest. Pushing the child to remember something that had frightened her speechless did not sit well with him. But what other choice did he have? The gunmen had proved they weren't going to stop coming after them, and he feared they'd use his family as bait to get to him if needed.

Abby was the key. He desperately needed to know what the child had seen that night. And so far, all he knew for sure was that she'd seen someone other than her father through the Chat-Time link.

"Abby, did your daddy tell you he was in danger?"

The little girl nodded, then pressed her face more firmly against her mother. Paige sent him a sharp look. "I think that's enough, Miles. She's too upset."

"I'm sorry she's upset. Truly I am. But just a

couple more questions, can you do that for me, sweetheart? Please?"

There was a long pause before Abby turned her head to look at him. Her damp, reddened eyes twisted his gut. She sniffled loudly, then nodded.

He gave her another encouraging smile. "Was the person you saw with your daddy a man?"

There was a flicker of uncertainty but then her head bobbed up and down. *Yes*.

Miles thought back to the photograph he'd seen of Aaron Eastham. "Did he have a lot of hair on his head?"

Abby looked confused then shook her head.

"So he was bald? Hardly any hair on his head?"

She frowned and shook her head. Abby's expression was one of frustration, as if he wasn't asking the right question. She reached up and patted her head.

It took him a moment to realize what she might be trying to tell him. "Was he wearing a hat?"

This time she nodded and put her hand over her nose and mouth.

A ski mask.

His hopes plummeted to the soles of his feet. The man who'd attacked Travis Olson had worn a mask.

Which meant Abby couldn't identify him. They were no closer to figuring out who was coming after them.

* * *

Cradling Abby close, Paige watched a myriad of emotions playing across Miles's ruggedly handsome face. She understood he was worried about his family, but her first priority was her daughter.

"You've been a big help, sweetie," she crooned softly, against Abby's soft brown hair. "Thanks for answering our questions. Do you want to watch another movie now?"

Abby nodded, but didn't attempt to move away. Her face was turned toward Miles. Paige couldn't easily tell if her daughter was still looking at Miles or not.

As before, she had the distinct impression that Abby wanted the detective to guess what happened. That she wanted to tell them, but couldn't say the words.

Was the horror of what she'd witnessed keeping her silent? Or something else? Had the masked man threatened her daughter, making her drop the tablet?

"Yes, thank you, Abby," Miles said in a low, husky voice. He reached out and smoothed his hand tenderly down Abby's back. "You're a good girl."

Abby reached out and put her tiny hand on Miles's arm, almost as if she was trying to comfort him. Miles bent his head and kissed her hand, before moving away.

Tears pricked Paige's eyes at the way Miles treated her daughter. She was struck once again at how great he was with kids and what a wonderful father he'd be one day.

But she knew better than to speak her thoughts out loud.

Her heart ached for Abby. Now that Travis was dead, her little girl would grow up without a father.

Unless she remarried…

As soon as the thought formed in her mind, she shoved it away. Not an option, she told herself firmly. When it came to men, her instincts couldn't be trusted. She'd believed Travis's lies, and ended up brokenhearted and alone. No way was she ready to trust another man.

Although, if she was going to ever let another man into her heart, she could easily imagine him being someone like Miles Callahan.

But not now. Not when her daughter needed a steady, stable home environment. If things didn't work out, Abby would be crushed.

"Thanks, Paige," Miles said, interrupting her tumultuous thoughts.

She couldn't manage a smile. "You're welcome."

He stood and returned to the kitchen table where the information Jason had sent him remained scattered about. After a few minutes, Abby lifted her head, pushing her hair out of her eyes. Then her daughter scrambled over the sofa cushions to retrieve the television remote control, turning and handing it to Paige.

She took the remote and found the kids' channel again. This time, the movie wasn't animated, but Abby didn't seem to mind. Her daughter picked up Ellie, cuddling the toy close, her thumb making its way back into her mouth.

Realizing how much her daughter had regressed in the past few days was troubling. Paige told herself it could be worse, but somehow that didn't make her feel any better.

Once she was sure that Abby would be okay, Paige joined Miles. "I'm not sure going through this information is helping," she said, dropping into a chair with a weary sigh. "We haven't found anything useful yet."

Miles grimaced and sat back in his seat. "I hate feeling helpless. If anything happens to the two of you. Or my family..." His voice trailed off.

"I won't forgive myself if anything happens to your loved ones, either," she said softly. "Trust me, I know very well that you're only in this mess because of me."

"Not true. I was at your house looking for Travis because of Jason's murder." He shoved the paperwork out of the way in a rare flash of anger. "And

I'm in danger because Jason sent me all of this. Too bad it's all scientific gobbledygook."

The comment struck her as funny. Miles was smart, but apparently he didn't speak science. "How long were you and Jason friends?" she asked curiously.

"We were roommates in the dorm our freshman year." A hint of a smile twitched at his mouth. "We were complete opposites—I was outgoing and loved sports, and he was a shy science geek." The smile faded. "Jason introduced me to Dawn and Shelly, two girls in his microbiology class. The four of us became friends. Once we didn't have to live in the dorm anymore, Jason and I shared an apartment not far off campus."

"What about Dawn and Shelly? Did they live with you guys, too?"

"No. By the end of our freshman year, we'd paired up. Jason and Shelly were a couple, and Dawn and I started going out together, too. Dawn wanted to become a registered nurse."

The sadness in his eyes tugged at her heart. "Wanted to be? What happened?"

"She was diagnosed with leukemia right before graduation." His lips tightened in a thin line. "She fought hard and did her best to live her life to the fullest. I helped any way I could, especially in providing new experiences for her."

He fell silent, but she sensed he needed to talk this out. "Like what?"

"We hiked the Pacific Trail, did some parasailing and rode in a hot air balloon. She wanted to go hang gliding, too, but there wasn't time. Ten months after her first dose of chemotherapy, she was gone."

"Oh, Miles, I'm so sorry." She pulled her chair closer and reached for his hand, cradling it between hers. "That must have been terrible for you."

"Terrible for her," he corrected in a grim tone. "She died a week after her twenty-fifth birthday. Too young. Far too young."

Paige didn't know what to say to make him feel better. "She's in a better place now," she reminded him softly.

His expression turned stony. "Oh, yeah?" There was a definite challenge in his tone that basically said, *prove it*.

Too bad, she couldn't. Instead, she regarded him steadily for a long moment. "Miles, I know it's not always easy for us to understand God's plan. When Travis kept cheating on me, I wondered why God had let me make such a huge mistake. Then I realized that He'd given me Abby. When you told me that Travis was gone, I couldn't see why God would take Abby's father away. Why he'd expose my little girl to danger." She dropped her gaze to Miles's tanned, muscular forearm. "I still don't understand, to be perfectly honest. We've been running from the gunmen for three days now, yet when I think about how terrible that is, I also realize that God is the one keeping us safe."

She paused and shrugged. "All I can do is to continue praying for safety and guidance. It's not up to us to question God's plan. It is what it is."

Miles let out a long breath and curled his large fingers around her much smaller ones. "You may be right. The foundation of my faith was shaken by Dawn's death. But I have to admit that I've started praying again. Since the night I met you, Paige. Watching you pray with your daughter reminded me how important it is to stay connected with God. It was easier to pray for you and for Abby than to pray for myself."

She was touched by his revelation. "I'm glad." She rubbed her thumb over his. "I'm sure Dawn's glad you found your way back to your faith, too."

His gaze was thoughtful and a muscle ticked in his jaw, but he didn't say anything. She wondered if maybe Dawn's faith had fallen by the wayside, as well.

"Miles, even though your faith was a bit rocky over these past few years, you should know that God was still looking after you. Just like He'll be looking after your family."

"I hope so." A shadow of worry darkened his gaze, but then he smiled. "I guess my being there that night the gunman started shooting at your house must have been a big part of His plan."

"It was." Their gazes clashed and held for several long moments. Then she did something completely out of character.

She took off her glasses, leaned forward and kissed him.

TWELVE

Paige's kiss caught him off guard, but only for a moment. Then he drew her close, deepening the kiss, enjoying the warmth and comfort he experienced from having her in his arms.

When they finally drew apart, he rested his forehead against hers, struggling to breathe normally. She splayed her hand over his heart, and he wondered if she could feel the erratic beat of his pulse.

Miles knew he should feel self-conscious about spilling the truth about his relationship with Dawn and his struggles with his faith, but he didn't. Instead he felt lighter than he had in years.

Yet as much as he wanted nothing more than to kiss Paige again, he slowly lifted his head. "We need to stay focused here. I have to continue my investigation," he said, his voice gruff with regret.

"Oh, yes. Of course. I don't know what I was thinking." Paige looked embarrassed as she picked up her glasses and slipped them back on. Almost as if she were hiding behind the frames.

"I don't regret our kiss," he said, wanting to reassure her that he wasn't taking her gesture lightly. "To be honest, I've never told anyone, except for my pastor, about how I felt after Dawn died. Until now." He flashed her a crooked grin. "Thanks for listening and for helping me to keep things in perspective."

A genuine smile bloomed on her face and he was struck by how pretty she looked when she was happy. "Anytime, Miles. I'm glad I could be there for you."

He stroked the tip of his finger down her cheek. "Your ex was a fool to let you go. Just remember that his failures are not yours."

The happiness faded from her eyes and she shrugged. "I'll try, but it's difficult not to take his indiscretions personally."

"His mistakes, not yours," Miles repeated sternly. "He's the one who broke his promises to you, not the other way around."

"I know..." Sighing wistfully, she turned and looked at the paperwork scattered all over the table. "So. I guess we'd better get back to work."

Miles nodded, pulling his thoughts back to the issue at hand. He'd already gone through the stuff, but he kept coming back to the fact that Jason had sent this information to his PO box for a reason.

There had to be something buried in the documents that he was missing.

Something that would lead to the identity of the killer.

With renewed determination, he picked up reading where he'd left off. As he neared the end of the documents, he noticed the scientific jargon was broken up by lists of numbers.

He cocked his head, then shuffled through the documents to find the beginning. The numbers weren't present until the last three pages of the document.

They didn't appear to be formulas, although he was far from a math wizard. They almost looked to be some sort of computer code.

He blew out a frustrated sigh. Why would Jason send him encrypted documents? His buddy knew that numbers were about as far out of his area of expertise as you could get.

Wait a minute.

Miles pulled the three sheets of paper with the numbers on them. What if they weren't computer code but some other type of code?

Using the basic, A=1, B=2, and so forth didn't work. Figured. Trust Jason to make it complicated. Doing the alphabet backward didn't work, either.

A feeling of helplessness gripped him around

the throat. He had to figure out what these series of numbers meant. He just *had* to.

Then it hit him. What if he started with vowels, the most common letters of the alphabet? Once he understood which numbers corresponded with the vowels, he'd have a better chance of cracking the code.

If there really was a code. What if he was imagining the numbers meant something when they really didn't? What if this was nothing more than a waste of time and energy?

Miles glanced at his watch and decided to give it an hour. If he hadn't made any headway by then, he'd move on to something else.

Paige moved away from Miles, doing her best to ignore the butterflies in her stomach. She had no idea what she'd been thinking to kiss him like that. When she'd met Travis, he'd been the one to pursue her. She'd never initiated any intimacy and she was mortified that she had done so with Miles.

Kissing him was nice. More than nice. His musky scent still clung to her clothing. If she wasn't careful she'd lose more than her common sense before this nightmare was over.

She'd lose her heart, as well.

Enough, she told herself sternly. This wasn't the time or place to focus on her love life. She glanced his way and saw that Miles was working furiously on the information his friend had sent. Why he continued to go over the information was beyond her, since the documents hadn't provided any clues so far.

Turning toward her daughter, she wondered if there was a way to help Abby cope with whatever she'd seen. The little girl still hadn't said a single word since that very first night, but maybe there was another way Abby could express herself.

Drawing? Wasn't that what some psychologists called play therapy? She wasn't an expert, but thought it might be worth trying.

Anxious to do something constructive, Paige quickly riffled through the cabinets, searching for paper and crayons or colored pencils. The kitchen didn't have anything like that, but when she walked down the hallway to the room that was obviously used as an office, she found exactly what she needed.

Paige brought the paper and colored pencils into the living room and fanned them out on the coffee table. Abby perked up, looking excited to have something to do other than watching cartoons.

"Would you like to draw pictures with me?" Paige asked, sitting cross-legged on the floor.

Abby nodded and settled in across the table from her. She picked up a black pencil and began drawing.

Paige kept an eye on her daughter's picture, a bit surprised when she realized Abby was drawing what looked to be a square structure.

"Oh, how pretty. Is that a picture of our house?" Paige asked.

Abby nodded, but didn't look up. Her forehead was puckered with concentration, as if she were working on a masterpiece.

The way her daughter worked so intently on her picture made Paige frown with concern. She wanted to ask more questions, but did her best to be patient enough to let Abby finish her drawing.

Time ticked by as her daughter seemed lost in a world of her own, picking up different colored pencils to add to her picture. Soon Paige recognized the pink curtains hanging at the window and the brown desk in Abby's bedroom.

Outside the house, Abby drew a large rectangle, then put a stick figure in the middle of it, adding short yellow hair. Travis? Maybe. Suddenly Abby drew a large black X over the stick figure's mouth. Paige swallowed a gasp. Abby looked up at her, wide green eyes tortured with the need for her mother to understand.

Paige tried to wrap her mind around what the

X meant. "Is this Daddy?" she asked hoarsely, tapping the yellow-haired stick figure.

Abby nodded, her gaze expectant.

"You saw Daddy on the tablet through the ChatTime link." Again, Abby nodded, but this time a sense of exasperation was in the child's gaze.

"Did someone have their hand over Daddy's mouth so he couldn't talk?"

Abby frowned and shook her head.

Paige tried again. "Did Daddy tell you to be quiet because someone might be listening?"

There was a flash of confusion, but then Abby shook her head. No.

"Is it that Daddy couldn't talk for some reason?"

This time Abby nodded, but her expression remained serious, as if there was more. She bent over the paper again and this time she drew a black sideways L-shaped thing.

A chill snaked down Paige's spine and she willed her voice to remain steady. "Is that a gun?"

Abby nodded and pushed the paper away as if she didn't want to draw any more.

"The man with the mask over his face had a gun?" Paige asked, trying to clarify. When Abby nodded, she added, "Was there more than one person?"

Abby shook her head.

Paige couldn't bring herself to ask if the man wearing the ski mask had shot Travis with the gun while Abby watched. She didn't think so, since her daughter hadn't drawn anything indicating blood or some kind of violence.

Just the large X over the stick figure's mouth.

She wasn't sure what the X meant, but it was clearly traumatic enough that her daughter hadn't spoken a word since seeing her daddy.

And Paige could only hope her silence wasn't permanent.

"I think I have it," Miles said with excitement. He looked over to where Paige was drawing with her daughter. "I cracked the code."

"Code?" Paige blinked in surprise and rose to her feet. She quickly came over to see what he meant. "Are you sure?"

"I'm sure." Miles hated to admit how long it had taken him to figure out Jason's encrypted message. "Look at this. Using the first five numbers backward matches up with the vowels. And the numbers 767 break up the words. This first sequence of numbers spells out this sentence: *I found and corrected the error in the robotic design.*"

Paige's expression was skeptical. "You really think that's what Jason was trying to tell you?"

"It's the only thing that makes sense." Miles

stared down at the remaining sequences of numbers. "Now that I cracked the code, getting the rest of the message should be easy."

He applied the corresponding letters to the numbers he'd identified, and then quickly wrote out the next sentence, the impact hitting him squarely in the gut.

"I'm in danger so I'm sending the information to you for safekeeping."

"The information contained on these sheets of paper?" Paige asked with a frown. "That doesn't make sense, because the stuff I read said something about being close to having the design, not that it was fully functional."

"Yeah, I know." Miles had gotten the same impression from reviewing the scientific jargon that Jason had sent him. "But there are more numbers here, so maybe he'll explain what he means."

"Maybe." She leaned close, her hair brushing his shoulder and her citrusy sent making it difficult to concentrate. "Keep going," she encouraged.

He didn't answer, since he was already in the process of doing just that. Deciphering the code was faster now that he was getting the hang of it. The next two sentences were long, though, and it took him several minutes to spell out all the words. When he finished, he had to read it through twice to comprehend what Jason was saying.

*There are rumors about Sci-Tech stealing from
ACE Intel and vice versa to the point I don't know
who to trust. The robotic design won't work without the missing link so I'm sending it to you for
safekeeping until we know who deserves to have
it.*

"The missing link?" Paige looked at him in
confusion. "What link? What's he talking about?"

"I have no idea." Miles scowled and shuffled
through the pages again. "I don't see a missing
link. He must have buried it in the information
somewhere?"

"He went through the trouble of creating a secret code to give us this much, why couldn't he
just spell out what exactly he meant in plain Eng-
lish? We don't know any more now than we did
before you managed to crack the code."

Paige's frustration mirrored his own. None of
this made a whole lot of sense. He put the papers
in order, determined to go through them one more
time. His eyes burned and his head throbbed from
his attempts to understand the detailed jargon.

"Maybe we should take a break for lunch," she
suggested. "That way you can start fresh in an
attempt to find the missing link."

"I guess." He wasn't particularly hungry, but
knew that Paige would want to keep to a normal meal schedule for Abby. He folded the dozen
sheets of paper in half and quickly stuffed them

back inside the padded envelope. He wasn't looking forward to going through them again for what felt like the hundredth time.

"I was only planning on having sandwiches. Is that okay?" Paige asked, retreating to the kitchen.

"Sure. Sounds good." He stood and stretched, trying to relieve the tense muscles of his neck and shoulders from being hunched over the kitchen table for so long. He glanced at the phone, wondering if he should check in with Mike, when Abby came over to him, holding up a picture as if she wanted him to have it.

"Is this for me?" he asked with a broad smile. "It's beautiful, thank you."

Abby frowned at him and shook her head.

"Oh, I should have realized you drew the pretty picture for your Mom."

Abby's scowl deepened and she stabbed her finger at the picture, as if he were stupid for not understanding. And maybe he was, because he truly didn't get what she wanted.

"She drew a picture of how she saw her daddy through the ChatTime link," Paige supplied helpfully as she opened a loaf of bread.

"You did?" He'd been so intent on cracking Jason's code that he hadn't paid any attention to what Abby and Paige were doing. He inspected the drawing carefully, realizing that the yellow-haired stick figure with the X over his mouth was her father.

The large X bothered him.

"She indicated that she only saw one person," Paige said. "And you can see she drew a G-U-N." She spelled the word, as if to prevent Abby from becoming upset.

After looking at the drawing again and identifying what must have been the gun, he went down on one knee so he could look at Abby's face. "This is a very good picture, sweetheart," he said gently. "Thank you for helping us to understand what happened that night."

Abby surprised him by throwing her arms around his neck and giving him a hug. He cradled her close, looking over the child's head to find Paige watching them, her eyes bright with unshed tears.

Miles pressed his lips to Abby's hair, wishing desperately that he could give the little girl the peace and safety she deserved.

It made him more determined than ever to find the missing link Jason had indicated.

Abby broke away from his embrace and rushed over to the kitchen to look expectantly up at her mother. Clearly Abby was ready for lunch, even something as mundane as peanut butter and jelly.

"I have turkey and roast beef," Paige said, setting Abby's sandwich aside.

"Roast beef." He walked over to the counter. "What do you need me to do?"

"There are glasses in the cupboard, will you pour some milk?"

"Sure." He did as she asked, and a few minutes later, lunch was ready.

Paige led the prayer and he found himself once again adding a silent plea that God would help Abby find her voice.

"Amen," he added, when Paige finished.

"Was there anything else in the PO box besides the envelope containing the papers?" Paige asked before popping a potato chip into her mouth.

He lifted a brow. "My regular mail was there. You know, bills, advertisements, that kind of thing. Why?"

"I keep wondering about the missing link he mentioned." She took a sip of her milk. "It would make more sense if it was a thing, rather than some obscure formula buried in the documents."

Miles took a bite of his sandwich, regarding her thoughtfully. "I'm not sure Jason would have risked sending it separately. Too easy to miss."

"Yeah, maybe." She didn't sound convinced.

He thought back to the morning he'd gone to the post office. He'd flipped through the mail pretty quickly, pouncing on the package from Jason almost to the exclusion to everything else.

What if he had missed a second package? The

moment the thought entered his mind, he dismissed it. No way would he have missed another package. Even a smaller one would have caught his eye.

The answer had to be within the information he already had. When they'd finished lunch, he carried their dirty dishes to the kitchen. But when he would have helped, Paige waved him off.

"I'll take care of it once I get Abby settled with a movie. She looks tired…I'm hoping she'll take a short nap."

Since he didn't know much about kids and their naptimes, he simply nodded. "All right, but if you want to leave the dishes to air dry, I'll take care of them later."

Abby must have heard the dreaded word nap, because suddenly she shoved her drawing off the kitchen table in a rare show of temper. Then she pushed the envelope with the papers tucked away inside off the table too, sending everything down onto the floor.

"Abby! What's gotten into you?" Paige chided, coming over to where the little girl was still sitting at the table. "I was going to let you watch a movie, but now I'm not so sure."

Abby kicked the table, then winced and pulled her foot up to rub her toes.

"She's tired," Miles soothed, coming over to pick the envelope and her drawing off the floor.

As he set the envelope down, he stared at it for a moment. Had he felt something? Setting Abby's drawing aside, he took the padded envelope in both hands and gently pressed on it.

There. His fingers found a miniscule ridge along the bottom left-hand corner of the envelope.

"I need a knife," he muttered to himself, reaching into his slacks and retrieving an old Boy Scout knife his father had given him as a kid.

Using the utmost care, he carefully separated the layers of the padded envelope. Then stared in shocked surprise at the small black SIM card that had been concealed in the Bubble Wrap.

He'd found Jason's missing link.

THIRTEEN

"What in the world?" Paige asked in a hushed tone, glancing up at Miles incredulously. "How did you find it?"

"I'm not sure," he admitted. "But obviously this is what Jason intended for me to keep safe. The way he'd used a code for his message makes sense. Even if the envelope had fallen into the wrong hands, it's unlikely that the SIM card would have been discovered. It was only by chance that I felt the ridge when I picked it up off the floor."

Apparently Abby's temper tantrum had worked to their advantage, this time.

"How does it work?" She leaned over to get a closer look at it. "Are these specific to a certain computer or phone?"

"I'm not sure." Miles grimaced and shrugged. "I don't want to try placing it in the computer, and risk damaging the information Jason must have put on it. I'd feel better if we had someone from the technical support team in our district to assist in reading what's on the card."

An inexplicable sense of dread gripped her by the throat. She swallowed hard. "Are you going to turn the SIM card over to your boss?"

Miles blew out a breath and shook his head. "Not yet, but I'll need to do something soon." He lifted his head and looked at her, and she wondered if her fear was reflected in her eyes. "We can't keep running forever, Paige. At some point, we'll need to trust the authorities."

No! Paige wanted to scream at the top of her lungs, but somehow managed to hold it together. "I understand what you're saying, but what do we really know?" she asked in what she hoped was a reasonable tone. "Jason's message stated that he wasn't sure who he could trust, and quite frankly we're in the exact same boat. I think it's best if we hold off calling your boss until we have a solid lead to act upon."

"You may be right, although it could be that the information on this SIM card is enough to blow the case wide open."

But what if it wasn't? Paige gripped the edge of the table, fighting the battering waves of irrational fear. She didn't want him to call his boss. For the first time since this entire nightmare began, she truly believed they were safe. Being in a private residence, where no one would think to look for them, made sense.

She couldn't bear the thought of once again accidentally revealing their location to the gunmen.

"Please, not yet," she begged. "Let's make sure that we don't tip anyone off as to where we are."

Miles didn't say anything for a long moment, but then he finally nodded. "All right, we'll hold off. For now."

She didn't appreciate the qualifier at the end of his statement, but she forced herself to turn away. She crossed over to turn the television back on, flipping through the channels until she found the cartoons.

Abby climbed onto the sofa and curled into the corner, pulling her stuffed elephant close. Paige stared at her baby, wishing once again, that they could just go home.

Miles came up to stand beside her and her heart betrayed her by skipping a beat. She didn't want to respond to him, not when she was beyond annoyed with him.

"I'll keep you safe," he murmured softly enough for her to hear, but not loud enough to reach Abby.

It was on the tip of her tongue to point out that he'd said that before, but then she felt a sense of shame.

None of this was his fault, any more than it was

her fault or Abby's. Look at how Miles had protected them, over and over again. And she firmly believed that God was watching over them, too.

"I know."

He slid his arm around her waist and she leaned against him for a moment, drawing strength from his nearness.

Maybe he was right about calling the authorities. They couldn't stay here indefinitely. Obviously the information on the SIM card was important.

Important enough to kill for.

It wasn't easy for Miles to step away from Paige. All he wanted was to continue holding her, breathing in her heady scent, but he needed to figure out his next steps. He'd agreed to hold off calling his boss for now, but that didn't mean he wasn't going to contact his family.

He knew both Mike and Mitch would help, yet at the same time, he didn't like pulling them off guard duty. He needed to know that his mother and grandmother were safe.

After tucking the SIM card back in the envelope, he stared at it for a long moment. He thought back to what Aaron Eastham had said about Karl stealing company secrets. That initial theft had happened years ago, but things had heated up now because his buddy Jason had found and fixed the error. Whoever ended up with the information stored on the SIM card would be in a position to bring the new robotic technology to market.

In all his years working homicide, he knew that the basis for almost every single crime was money.

Pulling out a piece of paper, he began jotting notes, the way he normally did while working a case.

Jason died on Monday night. The coroner's office claimed Travis Olson was killed on Monday, too, but he didn't believe that. He thought it was more likely that Travis died on Tuesday night, not too long after he'd connected with his daughter through ChatTime.

Miles tugged the envelope closer, peering at the time stamp from the post office. Jason had sent the envelope to him on Monday, obviously because his buddy knew he was in danger. And Jason hadn't wanted the SIM card to fall into the wrong hands.

He tapped his pencil on the tabletop, trying to figure out the timeline of events. Jason worked for Sci-Tech on the highly confidential project, which meant that the information belonged to owner Karl Rogers.

Why would Karl want to kill Jason and Travis?

It wasn't likely that either one of them threatened to take the information back to ACE Intel.

Why would they? Sci-Tech paid their salaries. When the robotic technology went to market, both Jason and Travis would be known as the inventors of the product.

Was it possible Karl Rogers didn't want to share the limelight with his research team? He grimaced, supposing it was possible, but it was not logical. Rogers would be more interested in having his company, Sci-Tech, bringing in money from the sale.

All of which brought him back to ACE Intel. If Aaron Eastham knew that Karl's team had finalized the robotic technology, he'd have no chance of gaining back the market share he'd lost.

He drew a circle around Aaron Connor Eastham's name. The owner of ACE Intel had to be the missing piece of the puzzle, but the black sedan with tinted windows had been owned by Sci-Tech, not ACE Intel.

Miles straightened in his seat as a wave of adrenaline hit hard. Unless there was someone else in Sci-Tech on Eastham's payroll. What had Eastham said? He'd haul Rogers back to court the minute he could prove that the termination agreement had been faked?

The cogs in the legal system churned slowly, too slowly to prevent Karl Rogers from making a boatload of cash off the new technology. Maybe Eastham decided to go with a more direct route.

Like stealing the technology back from Sci-Tech.

He grimaced, because his theory didn't explain why Eastham would kill Karl's research team. He'd almost expect Eastham to go after the owner himself, rather than Karl Rogers's employed researchers.

Opening the computer he typed *Aaron Connor Eastham* into the search engine. It took some digging to get some of his personal information, but it didn't take long for Miles to discover that Eastham had an ex-wife, Sarah Bentley, and no kids. According to the court document he'd uncovered, Eastham had been divorced for five years.

Wait a minute. Miles scowled at the date. The divorce had taken place within a month of Karl Rogers opening Sci-Tech.

The timing was interesting, but even though Miles stared at the date for several long minutes, he couldn't figure out how the two could possibly be related.

For all he knew, Sarah might not have any say-so in Eastham's business. The two had only been married for six years, and Eastham had owned the company prior to their marriage, so she likely didn't have an access to the income as a result of the divorce. And since they had no children there wasn't any child support, either.

He turned his attention to Karl Rogers. Rogers was also divorced with no children. Only Rogers's divorce was more recent, within the past three years.

The name of his ex-wife jumped out at Miles. Sasha Jorgensen.

According to Paige, one of Travis's more recent girlfriends was Sasha. What were the chances of that?

Not very likely.

Was it really possible that Travis Olson had been so bold as to date the owner's ex-wife?

Unbelievable.

For the first time since this ordeal started, it occurred to Miles that Travis Olson's death might not be connected to the SIM card Jason had sent him, after all. In fact, it was far more likely that Travis had died because of his affair with Sasha.

Would Rogers hire a masked man to kill Travis?

But if that was the case, then he still couldn't say for sure why Jason had been murdered. To get the SIM card, sure, but at whose hand?

The only logical explanation was that Aaron Connor Eastham had somehow learned of the work Jason had done in fixing the technology and had become determined to steal it back.

Now, Miles just needed to find a way to prove it.

The rest of the afternoon seemed to pass in slow motion. Paige wondered if it was because she was dreading the moment Miles told her they'd need to contact the authorities.

Abby had dozed for a bit, and when she awoke she actually looked as if she might say something, but then had simply pointed to the colored pencils, indicating she wanted to draw some more.

Paige pulled out fresh paper for Abby, wondering if the little girl was going to draw more images from the night Travis had contacted her through the ChatTime link. As much as Paige wanted her daughter to heal from the trauma, she was second-guessing her thought process of encouraging Abby to draw out her memories.

Maybe the past was better left alone.

When she looked at Abby's drawing, she realized her daughter was practicing her letters. Paige knew that Abby was learning to write her name and other simple words in her pre-kindergarten school program. Since Abby had only just turned five last month, she wasn't in an all-day kindergarten class yet. Normally Abby attended pre-K three days a week.

Except for this week.

Across the top of the page, Abby was writing several letters in a row creating the word DOT.

Hmm. Was there a child named Dot in preschool? The girls Abby talked about the most were Kate and Lucy. No one named Dot or Dorothy.

Then Abby put the letter N after DOT, which didn't make sense. Then she wrote the letters TAL. Again, Paige had no idea what those letters meant.

"Are these names of your friends from school?" Paige asked, pointing at the two clusters of letters.

Abby shook her head. She pointed at the letters, then ran over to the kitchen table and picked up her drawing of the stick man with a large X over his mouth. Abby pointed to the image of her father, then back at the letters.

DOTN TAL

Paige repeated them several times before they hit her like a brick.

Don't tell.

Goose bumps raised up on her arms as she finally understood the message Abby was trying to get across. Paige looked at her daughter. "Did your daddy say, *Don't tell*?"

Abby nodded, her tiny shoulders slumping as if a huge weight had been lifted off them. Paige reached out and gathered her daughter close.

The little girl pressed her face against Paige's neck and her heart wrenched when she felt the dampness of her daughter's tears.

"Shh. It's okay, sweetie. You don't have to keep secrets anymore. You can talk to us now, the danger is over." Even as she said the words, she realized they weren't exactly true.

The danger wasn't over. Not yet. It wouldn't be over until the gunmen who were hunting them down were arrested and tossed in jail.

"Something wrong?" Miles asked, rising to his feet and crossing over toward them.

"I'm trying to reassure Abby that she doesn't have to keep silent anymore." She gestured to the words Abby had written. "I'm pretty sure she heard Travis say *don't tell.*"

Miles was silent for a moment before he shook his head. "There's no reason for him to say that to a masked man. I wonder if he really said, *I won't tell.*"

She grimaced and nodded. "You could be right. She's only five years old. She may have misunderstood."

Miles dropped onto the sofa beside her and lightly stroked Abby's back. "This is a good sign, Paige. She's opening up, going to great lengths to help us understand what happened that night. She's a brave little girl."

Tears pricked Paige's eyes again, and she subtly swiped at them, wryly realizing that she hadn't cried this much since her divorce. "Yes, she is. Brave and smart."

"Listen, Paige, I found out that Karl Rogers, the

owner of Sci-Tech, was once married to a woman named Sasha. Do you think Travis would be so bold as to date his boss's ex-wife?"

She closed her eyes and drew in a deep breath. "Yes, I believe he would."

Miles let out a low whistle. "He likes playing with fire, huh?"

She kissed Abby's temple, her daughter's eyes were closed as if she'd fallen asleep, and forced herself to meet Miles's gaze. "You have to understand that Travis doesn't have basic common sense when it comes to women," she whispered. "He doesn't see the boundaries others think of as normal. He can also be very charming, making the woman he's with feel like she's the only one that matters. When, in fact, nothing could be further from the truth." She paused, then shrugged. "He cheated on me, and I'm sure he cheated on all the other women he dated after our divorce. It would never occur to him to consider the ex-wife of his boss as off-limits."

Miles nodded grimly. "Remember what I told you, Paige. His failures are not yours."

"I'm trying." She rocked back and forth with Abby, glad that her daughter's silent crying had stopped and that she was getting a bit of rest. "Do you think the attack on Travis is related to his boss, rather than the SIM card?"

"I think we have to consider the possibility." He

watched her for what seemed like endless minutes. "I've considered a couple of theories, but what I don't have is any proof. Except for the SIM card."

The card that they couldn't risk trying to read for fear of damaging it.

"You want to call your boss, don't you?" It was a statement not a question.

"Not my boss, but a detective who is also working the case." Miles leaned forward, his gaze imploring her to keep an open mind. "When we were at the other hotel, I called my boss, Captain O'Dell, directly. I've always trusted him, but I can't ignore the fact that he could have found a way to trace my disposable phone from that call."

Her mouth went dry. "What if your detective friend did the same thing?"

He shook his head. "That's just it, when I contacted Detective Krantz, I went through dispatch. I never gave her the opportunity to trace the number."

Her? Paige hadn't realized that Detective Krantz was a woman, not that it should matter one way or the other. She couldn't be jealous of a cop. Of anyone, for that matter.

Miles didn't belong to her.

She pushed those ridiculous thoughts away. "There must be other ways to trace disposable phones," she protested.

"Yes, but not as easily. There are ways to triangulate the signal, but that takes sophisticated equipment."

She tried to come up with another reason not to make the call, but she couldn't. Other than the fact she didn't want to.

"If you think that's what we need to do, then I'm okay with it." She was proud of how matter-of-fact she sounded. Good thing Miles couldn't tell how fast and erratically her heart was beating.

"Do you want me to meet her somewhere else? I can ask Mike or Mitch to stay here with you."

She remembered how Miles had instructed his brothers to watch out for his family. Dragging either one of them away would potentially leave his mother and grandmother alone and vulnerable.

"No, it's fine, I know they're keeping a close eye on your mother and grandmother." She glanced around the interior of the house. "We're in the middle of a family-friendly neighborhood, with houses on either side of us. We'll be safe here."

"Are you sure?" he asked, searching her gaze.

She smiled, liking the way he took her feelings into consideration. Something Travis had rarely done. Miles didn't belong to her, but staying with him over the past few days had shown her what the components of a good relationship should have.

Respect. Honesty. Caring. Partnership.

And *love*. Most of all, love.

She dropped her gaze, not wanting him to realize how close she was to falling in love with him.

"I'm sure." Abby shifted and blinked sleepily, turning her head so she could look at Miles. Paige stroked her back again reassuringly. "Do you think you'll meet with her tonight or tomorrow?" Secretly she was hoping for the latter.

"Depends on when I can connect with her." Miles smiled at Abby, then stood up and returned to the kitchen. He took the envelope and the paperwork and tucked them into a drawer before he picked up the phone.

"So, Abby, what do you think?" Paige asked her daughter. "Do you want to draw some more or watch TV?"

Abby's answer was to hand her the remote.

She could hear Miles on the phone with the detective as Paige found yet another children's movie for Abby to watch. Despite her anxiety, she told herself that it was probably best that the SIM card would be turned over to the police.

Maybe this nightmare would be over in a couple of days, and she'd be allowed to return home by the weekend. Once their life was back to normal, she'd find a way to tell her daughter that her daddy was with God.

"Detective Krantz is on her way," Miles said.

"I'm going to talk things over with her before I hand anything over, so it may take a while."

"Okay. Maybe you should call one of your brothers, too?"

He shrugged. "No need."

She wanted to argue, but knew it would be useless. When the doorbell rang fifteen minutes later, she instinctively stood up but Miles shooed her away. "I'll get it."

Inexplicably nervous, she stood in front of the sofa, twisting her fingers together. Miles opened the door and a tall blonde stood on the other side, wearing a long black coat over what looked to be a dark-colored jacket and slacks.

Paige recognized her immediately. "Sasha? What are you doing here?" She stared at the woman she'd seen hanging on her ex-husband's arm about three weeks ago. When had she become a cop? Had she always been a cop? Even when she was seeing Travis?

And then she saw the gun in Sasha's hand, pointing directly at the center of Miles's chest and knew that they were in terrible trouble.

FOURTEEN

The moment he heard Paige say "Sasha" was the same moment he saw the gun and knew that he'd messed up.

Big time.

"Back up, Callahan," Krantz said in a curt tone. "And keep your hands where I can see them."

Feeling sick to his stomach at how he'd trusted the wrong person, he held his hands up, palms facing outward as he took one step back, and then another, trying to angle himself so that he was in front of Paige and Abby.

This was his fault, not theirs, and he prayed for God to keep them both safe.

"So you've been the one behind this all along," he said, stalling for time. Maybe if he could get Krantz to relax a bit, he could overpower her in an attempt to get her gun, since his was tucked inside the pocket of his black leather jacket, which at the moment seemed as far away as the moon. "Did you kill Jason and Travis?"

Krantz stepped inside the Parkers' home and closed the door behind her. He didn't dare look back at Paige and Abby, but kept his gaze centered on the threat in front of him. She didn't bother answering his question. "Where's the information Whitfield sent to you?"

Miles swallowed hard, knowing that he couldn't afford to give her the SIM card. It might be the only bargaining chip he had at his disposal.

And he'd use it to get Paige and Abby to safety, if at all possible.

"I left it somewhere safe. I guess that's why you tossed my house, huh?" He made sure that he didn't so much as glance toward the kitchen, and prayed Paige and Abby wouldn't, either. "Pretty smart to call in the break-in and then work it as a burglary," he continued in a conversational tone.

"Yeah, I'm smarter than you any day of the week. Too bad most men only care about how I look." Krantz's expression turned to disgust. "Idiots."

"Why are you doing this?" he asked in an attempt to keep her attention on him, in case there was a way Paige and Abby could slip down the hall to safety. "You're a detective with the police department, why give that up?"

Lisa Krantz let out a harsh laugh. "Why else? Money. Do you have any idea how important that information is that was sent to you? How much it's worth?"

"Come on, Krantz, it can't be enough to forfeit your pension."

She let out the edgy laugh again, and the sound grated on his nerves like fingernails dragging down a chalkboard. "I've only been with the force for five years, do you really think I want to give it another twenty? Not hardly. I only joined the PD in the first place so that I could leverage my position in order to get what I really wanted." She gestured with the gun. "And what I want is what Jason Whitfield sent you. He was brilliant, I'll give him that, but now the information he created will belong to me."

"You? Or the person that hired you?" Miles estimated the distance between them as four feet, maybe five. Too risky to rush her now, but if he lied about where he had the information, he might have a chance. "Who are you working for? Since you divorced Karl Rogers, I'm betting you're on Aaron Eastham's payroll."

The flicker of surprise in her eyes gave him a sense of satisfaction. "My, my, you have been busy, haven't you, Callahan? Too bad you're one of the good guys who actually believe in upholding the law."

"Yeah, about that. You need to know that before I called you, I contacted the captain. He knows

I'm with you right now." Miles continued. "Killing us isn't the answer."

"Where's the information?" Krantz darted a glance around the room, as if it might be out in plain sight. Thankfully he'd decided at the last minute to put it away.

"I'll take you to the place where I left it, as long as you let Paige and Abby go."

Krantz's gaze narrowed and he held his breath when she tightened her index finger on the trigger. "Don't lie to me, Callahan. Do you think I'm stupid? You've been on the run since the night we hit Olson's house. In fact, we almost had you at that last hotel. There's no way you left the information behind. Get it. Now."

He didn't move, even though his heart sank at the thought of her calling in reinforcements. Actually, he was surprised she'd come without them. Unless they were waiting outside. If so, he couldn't afford to risk sending Paige out there. "Okay, I tucked the information away somewhere in the kitchen, so it may take me a minute to find it."

"Yeah, right." Krantz took a step toward him, holding her weapon level. "You're going directly to the spot where you hid the paperwork and if I see you reach for any kind of weapon, I'll shoot you in the kneecap."

"I understand." He walked backward toward

the kitchen area, keeping his gaze focused on Krantz. He didn't trust her. For all he knew, she might shoot either Paige or Abby just to make a point.

In fact, he was very much afraid that none of them were going to make it out of here alive.

Paige stayed directly in front of Abby, hoping that if Sasha…or Lisa Krantz—who knew which one was her real name?—didn't see her little girl, she wouldn't hurt her.

She noticed the way Miles stood protectively in front of her, too, but he wasn't bulletproof. She appreciated the fact that he was stalling for time, but despite what he was telling Krantz, he really hadn't called his boss or his brothers. No one was coming to their rescue.

Sooner or later, Krantz would start shooting.

And by the time the neighbors heard the sound of gunfire and called the police, they'd all be dead.

Please, Lord, please spare my daughter's life!

Paige risked a glance over her shoulder at Abby, who was watching with wide, frightened eyes. Abby must have picked up on the tension between the adults, and for once, Paige was glad that the little girl wasn't talking.

"Hide behind the sofa," she whispered in a

voice so soft she couldn't be sure that Abby could even hear her.

Her daughter stared at her for a long minute, then eased off the couch and crouched down on the floor. Then she crawled around the edge of the sofa, dragging Ellie with her.

Paige slowly inched backward, using the sofa cushion as a guide, toward the spot where she'd told Abby to hide. Maybe, just maybe, she could scoop the child up and make a run for it out the back of the house.

She didn't want to leave Miles behind, but at least he had the SIM card to use as leverage. And there was also the possibility that he'd be able to fight Krantz for the gun if she and Abby were someplace safe.

Taking another minute step back, then another, she finally reached the end of the sofa. She almost smiled when she saw that Abby had made herself as small a target as possible, her body curled around the stuffed animal. Slipping sideways, Paige stood right behind Abby, gauging the pathway leading down the hallway to the bedrooms.

When Miles agreed to hand over the paperwork and began walking backward toward the kitchen, she froze, her heart thundering in her chest, feeling like a deer caught in the headlights. It took every ounce of strength she possessed not to shout *No!* at the top of her lungs.

But then she noticed how Krantz's attention remained focused on Miles, as if she and Abby didn't exist. Paige released her breath in a sound-less sigh.

But they weren't out of danger yet, not by a long shot.

For a moment she stared at the phone, then told herself to forget it. It was located on the kitchen counter, too close to Krantz to be of any use, since both Krantz and Miles were making their way in that same direction.

Then she remembered the second phone located in the master bedroom. She'd noticed it when she made a quick walk-through of the house.

A wave of hope and adrenaline washed over her. If she could get to the bedroom and dial 911, they'd have at least a chance of help arriving in time.

But only if she moved quickly. Miles was still asking questions as he finally reached the middle drawer where he'd stashed the envelope.

There wasn't a moment to waste. She picked Abby up and rushed toward the hallway.

"Stop! Where do you think you're going?" Krantz demanded.

"Abby needs the bathroom. Unless you want a mess to clean up?" Paige didn't stop, but contin-ued down the hall. The master bedroom had its own small bathroom, but she didn't go in there.

Instead she crossed right over to the phone on the nightstand. She picked up the receiver and punched 911.

The ringing seemed incredibly loud, so she scrambled to find the mute button. When she heard the dispatcher answer, she unmuted the phone enough to whisper, "Send help, we're being held at gunpoint," before pushing the mute button again.

Making sure the phone remained on, she placed the receiver on the floor and kicked it under the bed, where hopefully Krantz wouldn't notice. Then she swung back toward the bathroom.

"Get out here!" Krantz yelled, and the way her voice grew louder, Paige knew that she was coming down the hall. She ducked into the bathroom, took a deep breath to calm her racing heart, before pretending to come out, still carrying her daughter, as Krantz pushed Miles into the bedroom.

"I'm sorry, but she's only five." Paige moved over to stand beside Miles, praying that the emergency dispatcher had already put out a call for help. What was the typical response time? Five minutes? Ten? "She's fine now. We can go back into the kitchen."

"Enough stalling!" Krantz's voice lashed like a whip. "I only need Callahan here to get the paperwork. You and the kid are just added baggage. I can just as easily get rid of you both, right now."

Paige's mouth went desert dry with fear. "I know. I'm sorry." She couldn't hide the tremor in her voice. "Please don't hurt my baby." She braced herself, wondering if her attempt to get help had only backfired. If Krantz decided to kill them...

She couldn't bear to think about it.

"Listen, you want the papers Jason sent me?" Miles interrupted, drawing Krantz's attention. "Then let's get them. Right now." He stepped forward even though Krantz still blocked the doorway. "I'll even show you the code he used to give us additional information."

"Code?" Krantz lifted her eyebrows in surprise and finally stepped back from the doorway. "Move it. And no more running off to the bathroom without my permission, understand?"

Paige didn't breathe normally until they were back in the main area of the house and even then, her knees still shook with the aftermath of what she'd done.

Miles went into the kitchen and pulled out the middle drawer, then tugged the paperwork out of the envelope.

"I'll show you the code." He flipped through the pages to the area where he'd found the sequence of numbers. Paige tuned him out when he went into great detail explaining how he'd used the vowels to figure out the message.

A small green light flashing on the phone sitting on the counter, caught her eye.

It took a minute for her to realize the light was an indicator that the phone was in use.

Blood drained from her face as the implication hit hard. The phone was right there, in plain sight. What if Krantz saw it? The light would prove that Paige's little jaunt to the bedroom was nothing more than a ruse to call for help.

And now that Miles had handed over the paperwork, there was nothing to prevent the detective from killing them all, right here, right now.

A bead of sweat rolled down the center of his spine, but Miles did his best to ignore it. He had no idea why Paige had risked running to the bedroom like that, especially since he'd been doing everything in his power to keep Krantz's attention focused on him and away from the two of them.

Time was running out. So far, stalling wasn't working very well. Only thirteen minutes had passed since Krantz had shown up at the front door. If he talked long enough, he might be able to eke out another five minutes.

But then what?

"Hey, what's with the missing link?" Krantz demanded, with a deep scowl marring her cold yet classically beautiful features. "Travis told me that Jason had figured out the robotic sequence.

That he'd completed the design. That's when we made our move."

"So, you were working with Travis?" he asked.

"Yes. He was riding Jason and told me that Jason had found a way to make it work. But then Travis got greedy. No way was I going to allow him to take more than his fair share, so I had one of my guys grab him. Travis claimed he wouldn't tell Karl my plan, but I knew he was lying. I took care of him, then realized he'd activated the Chat-Time link and the kid and her mother had over-heard what happened. Thankfully I had two guys in the area, and I ordered them to tie up the loose ends." Her smile lacked even one iota of warmth. "Don't push me, Callahan. I know Whitfield sent you the designs. Explain what this missing link means."

Miles spread his hands wide. "Hey, you know as much as I do now. In fact, I'll be honest, most of the information Jason included in these twelve pages was way over my head. It's all scientific mumbo jumbo. The missing link is probably in there somewhere."

Her scowl deepened. "You didn't find it?"

"No. But I'm sure another scientist could fig-ure it out. Maybe you shouldn't have killed Jason until you knew you had his designs."

"We did have them, but the sneak pulled a fast one by only giving us partial designs. I knew he had to have done something with the rest, and of course who else would Whitfield send them to but his best friend and former college roommate, Miles Callahan?"

He ignored her mocking tone. "I gave you what he sent me, so I don't know what else you want me to do." Miles tried not to stare at her weapon, even as he gauged his ability to snatch it out of her grasp.

Krantz stared at him, then gestured again with the gun. "Fold those together and put them back in the envelope."

Placing the papers back in the envelope where the SIM card was still hidden was the last thing he wanted to do, so he didn't reach for them. "Maybe you should read through them for yourself, make sure you have all the pages."

She glanced at the paperwork again, for just a fraction of a second, and he used the moment to surge forward, grasping her right wrist and forcing the muzzle of the gun up toward the ceiling.

Unfortunately, Krantz was a trained cop and stronger than she looked. She brought her knee up to hit him in the lower abdomen and swung at his head with her left hand. He managed to block her fist before she could hit him, but grunted in pain as her knee found its mark.

"Miles!" Paige screamed.

"Run! But not out the front, she might have

guys out there waiting!" Using his heavier frame to his advantage, he shoved Krantz backward, pinning her against the counter. She brought up her knee again, and he gritted his teeth against the blinding, searing pain.

A gunshot echoed loudly through the room, momentarily deafening him. He still had his wrist locked around her gun hand so the bullet disappeared into the ceiling.

There was a loud pounding on the front door, and Miles feared the worst—that anyone who might have been waiting for Krantz outside had heard the gunshots and come to investigate.

He squeezed his fingers tightly around her wrist in an attempt to get her to drop the gun. Her fierce gaze locked on his and he knew she was trying to hang on long enough for the gunmen to come to her rescue.

From the corner of his eye, he saw Paige edge around Krantz, then bend down to open cupboards. He knew she was likely searching for something heavy enough to use as a weapon.

"Get out," he urged. "Take Abby out the back. The gunmen are going to be in here any second."

"I'm not leaving you!" Paige pulled out a frying pan and swatted at Krantz. The blow caused her to loosen her grip.

Miles cranked Lisa's wrist to the side, prying

the weapon from her fingers. The front door burst open and more gunfire echoed through the house.

"MOMMY!" Abby's scream was loud enough to shatter glass, and when he risked a glance toward Paige, Krantz broke away from his grip.

But he managed to hang on to her gun. "Get down!" he shouted to Paige, as he opened fire on the gunmen who'd entered the living room. He hit one of them, sending the guy stumbling backward, but the second man flew forward, landing on his face. After a moment he realized the second gunman had been shot in the back.

His brother Mike edged around the door and Lisa Krantz ran straight for him.

"Look out! Krantz is one of them!"

Mike grabbed her and used Lisa's momentum to swing her around, planting her firmly up against the wall. Within seconds he'd snapped handcuffs around her wrists and taken a cloth out of his pocket and tied it across her mouth to keep her from screaming for help. Then he looked over at Miles. "Are you all right?"

"Yeah, I think so." Miles took one step toward Paige and Abby, but then his knees buckled and he sank to the floor.

"You're bleeding!" Paige crawled toward him, bringing Abby with her. The little girl was sobbing and saying *"Mommy, Mommy,"* over and over again. He wasn't sure if it was good or not that she'd broken her self-imposed silence.

The last thing he remembered seeing was Paige's face, streaked with tears, moments before he was engulfed in darkness.

FIFTEEN

"Help! We need an ambulance!" Paige placed the palm of one hand over the wound in Miles's shoulder in an attempt to slow down the bleeding, while holding on to her daughter with the other.

Poor Abby continued to say "Mommy" over and over again, and she did her best to reassure the little girl. "It's okay, sweetie, we're safe now. See? Miles's brother is here and he's going to make sure we're safe."

Abby gripped her so tightly around the neck that it was difficult to breathe, but Paige couldn't bring herself to loosen her baby's hold. The poor kid had been through so much trauma since that very first night when she'd seen her father being attacked through ChatTime. How much more could she take?

Paige didn't want to find out.

For now, the immediate threat was over. Although looking down at Miles's ashen features wasn't at all reassuring. What if he died as a result of his injury? Her heart squeezed painfully at the possibility.

Please, God, please heal Miles from his physical wounds and Abby from her emotional ones. Please?

"Are you all right?" Michael asked, coming down to kneel beside her. He'd taken a clean dishtowel out of one of the drawers and gently moved her hand out of the way so he could use the towel to apply pressure.

"Yes, we're fine. Did you call for an ambulance?" Paige fought to keep her voice steady. "He's lost so much blood..."

"Hear the sirens?" Michael flashed a crooked grin, but couldn't hide the concern in his eyes. "Both the police and the ambulance are pulling up now. He'll be okay, the Callahans are tough."

"How did you know to come here?" she asked as she realized Michael was there alone. Now that she thought about it, she found it incredible that both he and Miles had taken down the gunmen and cuffed Krantz without any other backup.

"I have a police scanner. I heard the 911 operator sending out the authorities to this address for a hostage situation." He glanced up at her with admiration in his eyes. "They said the caller was female. I'm not sure how you managed to get in touch with the emergency dispatcher, but it worked."

Paige was glad that her effort to get to the phone hadn't been for naught. If not for Miles's attempt to stall for time and her ability to make the call, she knew the outcome here could have been very different. "How did you get here before the police?"

"I was closer." Mike dropped his gaze to his brother. "I only wish I could have gotten here sooner."

"Me, too." The blood seeping through the dishtowel made her feel sick to her stomach. But before she could say anything more, two cops burst into the house.

"Lean on this," Mike instructed, before rising to his feet to face the officers. "I'm Michael Callahan and this is my brother, Detective Miles Callahan. The female detective I have cuffed and gagged is Lisa Krantz and I restrained her when she made a run for it because she's been holding these people hostage."

"Are you kidding me?" The officer looked between them incredulously. "She's a cop."

"Are we clear?" Two paramedics interrupted the discussion by coming in through the doorway, wheeling a gurney. "We hear there's an injured officer."

"Yes, the scene is secure. Please help my brother." Michael gestured for them to come around into the kitchen where Miles was stretched out on the floor.

Paige didn't want to leave Miles, but the paramedics edged her out of the way. She stumbled to her feet and joined Michael.

"Detective Krantz held you hostage?" The officer repeated, clearly not ready to buy their story. The way he kept glancing at Krantz was worrisome.

"Yes. I recognized her...she was dating my ex-husband, going by the name of Sasha," Paige said, hoping she could convince the officers not to let Lisa Krantz go. "I believe she's been sending gunmen after us for several days now, and unfortunately we trusted her enough to tell her we were here. She held us at gunpoint because she wanted information. Miles fought with her for the gun, and managed to shoot one of the gunmen who came in to rescue her. Mike shot the other one. The Callahans saved us, while Krantz has been the one behind this from the very beginning."

The officers exchanged a long look. "And who are you?"

"Paige Olson, and this is my daughter Abby. My ex-husband was Travis Olson, but he—" She stopped abruptly, belatedly remembering Abby was listening. She hitched the child higher on her hip, then continued. "He worked at Sci-Tech along with Jason Whitfield. Miles was investigating

Jason's murder when he came to my house to find Travis. Before he could even get to the door, we were under fire from a hidden gunman."

"I heard about that," the second officer said. The gold nametag over his pocket read Warner. "Gunshots were fired at a residence, but by the time the police arrived, the woman and child were gone."

"Miles saved our lives, Officer Warner. More than once. Michael, too."

"What kind of information was she looking for?" The first officer's nametag said his name was Yanko. "Do you have it?"

Paige glanced over at Michael, suddenly suspicious of Yanko's line of questioning. Maybe she was overreacting here, but how did she know if she could trust him?

If Detective Krantz was dirty, others could be, as well.

Michael must have understood her silent plea, because he quickly interjected. "There's a lot about this case that only Miles understands."

"We need to get this guy to the hospital, stat," the paramedic said in a loud voice, drawing their attention to Miles.

Paige whirled around, a hard lump lodging in her throat when she saw that Miles was lying on the gurney, pale and still.

"Go," Officer Warner said in a commanding

tone, stepping out of the way to make room for the gurney.

"Wait! Which hospital?" Paige asked, trailing behind.

"Trinity Medical Center," one of the paramedics answered, before they whisked Miles out the door.

"I'll take you," Michael promised. "Why don't you wash up a bit while I notify my family, okay?"

She nodded, grimacing at the dark redness staining her hands. She sent up a silent prayer, asking again for God to help heal Miles then turned toward the kitchen, and propped Abby on the edge of the counter while she quickly washed up.

"Hold on, now, you're not going anywhere until we're finished taking your statements," Officer Yanko said in a firm voice.

"Are you placing us under arrest?" Michael asked in a clipped tone.

Yanko flushed. "No, of course not. But we need to understand what happened here."

"I've already explained what happened, as did Mrs. Olson. We're both happy to cooperate, and will provide you complete statements as soon as we can. Right now, the woman and her child have been through a difficult ordeal. And I'm sure you can give us a few hours to make sure my brother is going to survive his injury."

After Paige finished washing her hands, she edged closer to the kitchen drawer where the padded envelope still remained. The paperwork was scattered all over the place, but all she really wanted right now was the SIM card.

Both officers were talking to Michael, and since neither one seemed to be paying any attention to her, she quickly slipped the SIM card out of the envelope and tucked it into the front pocket of her jeans.

"Mommy? Where's Miles?"

Abby's voice had returned! "Oh, sweetie, it's so good to hear you talking again. Miles is at the hospital, the doctors there are taking care of his ouchie. We'll go visit him as soon as we can, okay?"

"Okay." Abby stuck her thumb back into her mouth and rested her head on Paige's shoulder. Tears pricked her eyes, and she hoped and prayed that this meant that Abby was on the road to healing from the emotional upheavals they'd been through.

"I love you so much, Abby." She pressed a kiss to the little girl's cheek.

"I love you, too, Mommy."

Paige thought the words spoken by her daughter were the most beautiful sound she'd ever heard.

Now, if only she knew what was going on with Miles. Was he doing okay? Had he gone into surgery? She desperately needed to know, and with a pang, she realized she'd failed in her effort to keep from getting emotionally involved with him.

She cared about him. In fact, she was fairly certain she'd fallen in love with him.

Of course, she doubted he felt the same way, since he'd made it clear he wasn't interested in being a father. But at the very least, she needed to know that he would recover from this injury before she went back to her calm, peaceful, yet unbearably lonely life.

The hospital waiting room was crowded with Callahans. Just about everyone in the family had come except for Marc and Kari, but that was only because Kari was on bed rest due to her blood pressure being elevated. Michael had introduced Paige around, and while Mrs. Callahan and Nan eyed her with curious speculation, they treated her politely and no one questioned why she was there.

Paige stayed close by Michael's side, mostly because he was the brother she was most comfortable with. Gazing at Miles's family, the similarities in their facial features clearly showed they were related. Yet, they all looked a little different, too. Mitch had short blond hair, Michael wore his dark brown hair long, sometimes tied back, sometimes not. Yet each of the men seemed the strong, protective type.

Miles had been in surgery since they'd arrived about two hours ago and the waiting, not knowing what was happening, was killing her.

Abby had fallen asleep on her shoulder, so Paige held her close and remained seated so as not to disturb her.

"Your daughter's adorable." A woman with shoulder-length curly brown hair dropped into the seat beside her. Maddy Callahan. She and Matthew were twins, and she remembered Miles telling her that Maddy worked in the DA's office.

"Thank you." Paige rested her cheek against Abby's hair, grateful that the little girl was able to get some badly needed rest. "I hope we hear something about Miles soon."

"Yeah." Maddy's expression grew somber. "It wasn't that long ago that we were right here in this same spot, waiting to hear news about Marc. I'm not sure what it is, but my brothers seem to have a penchant for getting themselves shot while working their cases."

Paige swallowed hard, wondering if the Callahan family thought Miles's injury was her fault. She couldn't deny having some responsibility. "I'm sorry."

Maddy's eyebrows shot up in surprise. "Oh, you don't have to apologize. You and your daugh-

ter are the true innocent victims in this mess."
Maddy narrowed her gaze. "It's that Detective
Krantz who's at fault. Obviously the DA's office
isn't going to let me work this case because I'm
related to the victim, but still, there's *nothing* they
can do to keep me out of that courtroom when
that dirty cop goes before the judge."

Paige nodded, a little sad to realize she probably wouldn't see Miles again once she left the hospital. Their time together was over. She needed
to focus her energy on rebuilding her life, especially now that Travis was gone.

"So, how well do you know Miles?" Maddy
asked in a casual tone.

"I met him for the first time on Monday." Today
was Thursday. Four days. How was it possible
that she'd only known Miles for such a short time?

"Ah, well, I'm sure you've learned firsthand
how Miles tends to be a flirt, but you should know
that deep down, he's really a great guy."

A flirt? For a nanosecond her ex-husband's face
flashed into her mind, but then she remembered
how Miles had talked about Dawn, his college
sweetheart, losing her battle with cancer. Yeah,
Miles had kissed her, but he'd never been inap-
propriate with her. And he'd been nothing but
kind and caring with Abby.

So what if he had a reputation for being a flirt?
He was completely different from Travis.

In so many ways.

"Miles has never flirted with me," she told Maddy. "But I suspect that was mostly because we've been too busy running from gunmen trying to kill us."

"He hasn't?" Maddy looked surprised. "Huh. That's unusual. Personally, I've always thought Miles used his flirty approach toward women as an excuse to keep from getting too emotionally involved."

"I agree. Losing Dawn so young really affected him."

Now Maddy's jaw dropped. "He told you about her?"

Paige's cheeks grew warm as she realized she may have given Miles's sister the wrong impression about her relationship with Miles. "Well, yes, but only because we were talking about faith and God."

"Wow." Maddy looked as if she didn't know what to say.

Paige tried again. "Miles is a great guy and a good friend. I owe him a lot for saving my life and Abby's, too."

"Well, from what Mike tells me, you had a hand in getting ahold of the authorities, so we owe you a heartfelt thank-you, as well."

Paige didn't think her contribution was worth that much, but decided to drop the subject. Thankfully, Michael took that moment to cross over to them. "Hey, Maddy, do you think I can have a few minutes alone with Paige?"

"Sure, but keep in mind that Miles saw her first." Maddy winked at Paige before relinquishing her chair to her brother.

Now it was Paige's turn to gape like a fish. "Oh, uh, really, I don't know what she's talking about..."

"Oh, don't pay attention to Maddy," Michael said with a wave of his hand. "She's always trying to match us up with women, even though she complains bitterly when we give her feedback on her boyfriends."

Paige could only imagine what it was like for Maddy to grow up with five older brothers. "Yeah, I'm sure."

Michael lowered his voice, his mood turning more serious. "We'll have to give our formal statements to the authorities once we hear how Miles is doing. Is there anything you want to tell me? I got the sense back there that you didn't want to give Officer Warner the details of the information Krantz was looking for."

"Yes, actually. I want to give you this." She pulled the tiny SIM card out of her pocket, handing it over with a sense of relief. "Remember the day Miles went to the post office?" When Michael nodded, she gestured to the small card.

"The paperwork Jason sent in the padded envelope wasn't the real secret. We found that in the padding. Whatever information is on that SIM card is what Krantz was after."

"Did Miles figure out who she was working for?" He tucked the card into the pocket of his jeans.

She nodded. "Lisa Krantz used to be married to the owner of Sci-Tech, under a different name, but they divorced three years ago. Miles thought she was probably working for Aaron Connor Eastham, the owner of ACE Intel. She also claimed she was doing it for the money."

"ACE is Sci-Tech's biggest competitor. I found some interesting facts about how ACE Intel's net worth dropped from fifty million to less than one million when Sci-Tech opened up."

Millions? "No wonder she was so anxious to get her hands on that SIM card. If ACE gets the information and takes the technology to market, they stand to make all that money back."

"Yeah, and then some." Michael's expression was grim. "Keep in mind that the company was worth fifty million before they had the technology glitch solved. That amount could easily double, maybe even triple."

That kind of money was mind-boggling. And so far out of the realm of her day-to-day life that she couldn't even comprehend it. But at least this explained why Krantz hadn't hesitated to kill the people who got in her way.

Like Jason. And Travis.

She battled a wave of sadness at the fact Abby would never see her father again.

"I wonder if the information on this card will give us the proof we need to link Krantz to Eastham," Michael mused.

A chill snaked down her spine. "Even if it doesn't, they'll still arrest Aaron Eastham, right?"

"I hope so. Besides, technically this information belongs to Karl Rogers. Jason was working for Rogers when he figured out how to make it all work."

"Yeah, but Rogers violated his noncompete clause to open up Sci-Tech in the first place." All of this fighting between the two companies was beginning to give her a headache. "I guess it doesn't matter to me one way or the other, as long as we're no longer in danger."

"Yeah." Michael's expression was serious. "When we're finished here, I think it would be best if I take you and Abby to another motel. Just to be on the safe side."

That was the absolute last thing she wanted to do, but then again, there hadn't been time to get all the broken windows repaired so going home wasn't an option. "Okay."

"Mrs. Callahan?" A slender woman wearing

scrubs entered the waiting room. She was pretty with red hair pulled back in a ponytail, and young enough to make Paige wonder if she was a doctor in training.

"Yes?" Miles's mother and grandmother jumped out of their seats, and the rest of the siblings crowded close. Paige eased upright, taking care not to jostle Abby, and edged closer so that she could hear the news as well.

"I'm Dr. Gabriella Hawkins and I'm the trauma surgeon who operated on Detective Callahan. He lost a fair amount of blood, but overall he's in stable condition. The upper lobe of his right lung was damaged, so we had to remove it."

"Oh, no," Maddy murmured.

"It sounds worse than it is. The right lung actually has three lobes, so he shouldn't suffer any long-term damage from this." Dr. Hawkins glanced at her watch. "He's been in the post-anesthesia care unit for almost thirty minutes now. He'll be ready to move to a regular room in less than an hour."

"Thank you, Dr. Hawkins," Miles's mother said, reaching for the surgeon's hand. "Thank you for saving my son."

Dr. Hawkins smiled. "I'm glad I could be here for him." She moved as if to turn away, then swung back around to face the group. "Oh, by the way, who is Paige?"

The entire Callahan clan turned to look at her. "I'm Paige," she said self-consciously.

"Detective Callahan has been asking for you. I hope it's okay for me to let him know that you're here. He's been a handful for the nurses, keeps trying to get up and out of bed to come find you."

Her cheeks blazed with heat. "Of course. Please tell him I'm fine. That my daughter and I are both fine."

Dr. Hawkins's smile softened when Paige smoothed a hand down Abby's back. "I will. You can all see him once he's in his regular room, okay?"

Paige nodded, and there was a long moment of silence as the Callahan family digested that bit of information.

She hid her face against Abby's hair, her heart flooding with warm relief.

Miles was going to be all right.

And he wanted to see her, at least one last time.

SIXTEEN

"No drugs," Miles croaked in a hoarse voice. His throat felt like it was on fire, but he did his best to ignore it, his gaze locked on the nurse. "I mean it, no pain meds."

"We need to keep your pain at a manageable level," the nurse protested. "Trust me, if we don't, you'll be screaming in pain in a couple of hours."

Miles stared at her, grinding his teeth. "I don't want anything that makes my brain foggy," he repeated. "Don't you have over-the-counter types of pain meds here?"

"You can't swallow pills right after surgery." The nurse was eyeing him with exasperation, giving him the impression that he was her most difficult patient. "What if I only give you half the dose the doctor ordered? Will you try that?"

"Fine." His head was still woozy from the anesthetic agents they'd used during surgery, making it difficult enough to stay awake.

But he wanted, needed, to see for himself that Paige and Abby were all right.

The nurse must not have been kidding about using a half dose, because whatever she gave him didn't touch the pain. He might have zoned in and out a bit, though, because the next thing he knew, two people wearing scrubs were wheeling him to another location.

"What's my room number?" he asked, as they whisked him around a corner. From his position on the bed everything was a blur.

"You're in room 312 on the post-surgical unit," one of the scrub wearers responded.

He nodded and patiently waited as he was checked over one last time before they left him alone. He took several deep breaths, trying to shake off the lingering grogginess. A brief rap on his door had him turning his head in that direction.

"Miles?" The rush of relief was staggering when he saw Paige standing there, holding Abby. From the limpness in the little girl's arms and legs, he assumed she was asleep.

"Come in," he said, lifting his left hand off the bed. The amount of concentration and effort that took was pathetic. "How are you?"

Paige smiled and reached for his hand. "I'm pretty sure that's my line. You're the one who just got out of surgery. How are you feeling?"

"Better now that you're here," he acknowledged, enjoying the feeling of her hand in his. "I
was worried that you or Abby might have been
hit by a stray bullet or something."

"We're fine. Michael has been taking good care
of us."

A stab of jealousy hit hard, which was ridiculous. He should be glad his brother was there to
look after her, since obviously Miles couldn't.
"I'm glad."

Abby stirred in Paige's arms, and suddenly
lifted her head, blinking sleepily. "Miles?"

Hearing her speak his name was enough to
choke him up, and he swallowed hard and attempted a reassuring smile. "Hey, Abby, it's good
to see you."

"See, I told you Miles would be all right," Paige
said, shifting so that the little girl could see him
better, even in the low light of the hospital room.

"Miles," Abby repeated, holding out her arms
in his direction as if she wanted him to hold her.

"Easy, honey, he has a big ouchie on his shoulder," Paige cautioned. She awkwardly bent over
so that Abby could reach out and touch him.

Abby patted her hand gently against his face
and he cupped her tiny hand, pressing it against
his skin, savoring the moment. Then he pressed
his mouth to the center of her palm.

"All better soon?" Abby asked.

"Yes, sweetheart, I'm already feeling better now that you and your mom are here." Miles caught Paige's gaze, surprised by the sheen of tears in her eyes. "Hey, what's wrong?"

"Nothing." Paige hastily swiped at her eyes with her free hand and sniffled. "I'm just glad you're okay. I was so worried…" Her voice trailed off.

"Hey, don't underestimate the Callahans," he teased. "Nothing can keep us down for long."

That made her laugh. "Yeah, that's what I hear." Then her smile faded. "I better get going. I'm sure the rest of your family is anxious to see you, too. They insisted I come in first, but I know they're worried."

"Wait." He reached out a hand to stop her, lightly grasping her arm. There was a momentary flutter of panic in his chest at the thought of Paige and Abby being out there, alone. "Where are you staying tonight? You can't go home— your windows haven't been repaired yet."

"I know." She rested her hand over his and it was crazy how much that small gesture meant to him. "Michael thinks we should stay at a hotel for what's left of the night. The police need our formal statements tomorrow, anyway."

The tightness eased up a bit. "Yeah, okay. Good thinking."

"Get some rest, Miles."

He nodded but didn't want to let her go. "I will. But come back in the morning to see me, after you've finished with the police, okay?"

"Sure."

"Oh, and where's the SIM card?" He couldn't believe he hadn't asked about that first thing. Proof that his brain wasn't firing on all cylinders.

"Your brother has it, don't worry." She surprised him by leaning over and giving him a quick kiss on his cheek. "See you tomorrow."

"Good night." Miles watched her leave, hating the idea of her being in a hotel room without him. Which was just plain crazy as he wasn't able to protect her in his current condition.

A few minutes later, his mother and Nan came in to see him, followed by the rest of his family. Mike didn't stay long, but that was okay since he knew his brother was leaving to take care of Paige and Abby.

He loved his family, he really did, but after about thirty minutes of their fussing, he was exhausted. Oddly, the two people he found calming and relaxing were Paige and Abby.

Morning couldn't come soon enough.

Paige didn't sleep well that night, even though she knew they were safe and that Michael was stationed right next door.

His presence just wasn't as comforting as Miles's.

The day dawned bright and sunny. A rare warm front moving through the city brought temperatures in the 50-degree range, a nice change from the bitter coldness of the last few days. March had left like a lion and they were ready for April showers.

Paige fed Abby at the continental breakfast buffet, mentally steeling herself for the upcoming meeting with the police detectives assigned to follow up on the shooting incident at the Parkers' home.

Michael joined her at the table, his expression serious. "Mitch and I have been asking around. So far no one seems to know if Eastham's been arrested yet, apparently different jurisdictions are causing communication issues."

Her stomach knotted with tension, although she couldn't say she was surprised. "Are they working with the Chicago PD?"

Michael grimaced. "Yeah, from what I hear that's part of the holdup. Chicago PD doesn't seem to think there's enough evidence against him. They're not willing to believe the word of a dirty cop."

The knot in her stomach tightened, and she pushed her plate away, her appetite vanishing. "So, now what?"

"I'm not sure. I think, for now, we refrain from telling the police about the SIM card. I have a buddy who thinks he can look at whatever information Whitfield stored on it, and once we know we have the proof we need, then we'll hand it over."

"Okay." She didn't like the idea of holding back from the police, but she could agree with his logic.

Michael glanced at Abby. "My mom offered to watch Abby while we're at the police station."

An instinctive protest rose to her lips, but before she could say anything, Michael lifted a hand, stopping her.

"I know it won't be easy to leave her for a few hours, but it might be easier for you to speak frankly with the detectives without her listening in."

Assailed by indecision, she nibbled her lower lip. "I don't know how Abby will react around strangers," she hedged. "She's been through a lot of trauma over these past few days."

"I know." Michael's voice was gentle. "But my mom did raise six kids...I'm sure she can handle it. Besides, there's an old dollhouse of Maddy's that Mitch brought down from the attic last night. I'm sure she'd have a blast playing with it."

"Dolly?" Abby perked up, tuning in to the adult conversation.

"Well, all right, then." Paige told herself it would be good for her daughter to interact with other people in a normal environment after everything that had happened. Besides, she'd only be gone for a couple of hours at the most. "It's very nice of your mother to offer."

"Oh, don't thank us, yet. I think she's hoping to grill you about your relationship with Miles," Michael said with a quick grin.

She hoped her blush wasn't too noticeable. "There's nothing to tell. He saved our lives and almost died for his effort. I'm surprised she's not upset with me."

Michael rose to his feet and began clearing away the debris from their table. "She was the wife of a cop for a long time. She knows the risks and certainly doesn't blame you for what happened."

Maybe she should, Paige thought with a sigh. Then she remembered that Miles's dad was the police chief who was shot and killed while at the scene of an officer-involved shooting.

Yes, no doubt Mrs. Callahan knew the risks of being married to a lawman. Paige wondered what it would be like to watch someone you love go out on the job every day, knowing he'd be in danger. Yet, look at Travis, he'd been the director of research and development, but he'd gotten mixed up in something that had gotten him killed.

The best answer was to have faith. And she was

humbled by the thought of the Callahans' faith being strong enough to support jobs that served the community.

Detectives Schneider and Lipski were waiting in a small interrogation room when she and Michael arrived. Lipski took Michael into a separate room, while Schneider remained with her.

The questions started out simply enough, and Paige did her best to reiterate the events that had transpired in sequence, beginning with the gunshots fired at her house that very first night and how Miles had been there to help her escape. Sometimes Schneider interrupted her, but for the most part he let her talk and took copious notes.

He was particularly interested in how she'd recognized Detective Lisa Krantz as Sasha, one of the women her ex-husband had been dating.

"I saw them leaving Sci-Tech together, roughly three weeks ago," she explained. "He introduced her as Sasha, I don't remember a last name. But as a tall, strikingly beautiful blonde, she wasn't easy to forget."

"Is there any chance you could have been mistaken?" Detective Schneider pressed. "I mean, one brief meeting all those weeks ago…it would be easy to understand how a mistake could have been made."

She narrowed her gaze, her tone turning frosty.

"I didn't make a mistake. In fact, I called her Sasha when I saw her standing in the doorway, and she didn't deny it. Plus she admitted to knowing Travis, my ex-husband. She claimed she was working with him until he got too greedy. Then she was forced to silence him. She also admitted that she sent gunmen to my house to take care of the loose ends, meaning me and my daughter."

"And you took that to mean she killed him and attempted to kill you?"

"Wouldn't you? Especially since she was holding a gun on us when she said it." She was beginning to get annoyed with the detective and leaned forward in her chair, pinning him with a fierce look. "That woman made it clear she was going to kill us all, including my five-year-old daughter. A little girl who had done nothing wrong except be on the wrong side of a ChatTime link. If Miles hadn't gone after her, fighting to get her gun, she would have succeeded. As it was, Miles was shot by one of her thugs, nearly dying from his injury. That's what I know. And that's what you need to remember when she claims she's innocent."

"Okay, I hear you." Schneider was smart enough to back off in the face of her righteous anger. "We discovered that Lisa Krantz was actually Sasha Jorgensen's best friend in college. Krantz disappeared, and then resurfaced here in Milwaukee, and we believe Sasha stole her friend's identity to become a police officer."

Paige was stunned at the news. "I'm surprised she passed the background checks."

Schneider grimaced. "Someone dropped the ball there, but Lisa Krantz's background was squeaky clean so there was no way for us to know Sasha stole it. And we have reason to believe the real Lisa Krantz may be dead." He glanced down at his notes. "Is there anything else you can tell me?"

Paige sat back and picked through her jumbled memories. "When Miles asked if she was working for Aaron Eastham at ACE Intel, she didn't deny it, just made some crack about how busy he'd been investigating this case. But as I see it, that's the only thing that makes sense. Miles found out that Karl Rogers divorced a woman named Sasha three years ago and I believe she's still holding a grudge about that, and when you factor in the lure of big money, she decided to get what she must have felt was owed to her."

"You may have a point," Detective Schneider agreed. "We're in the process of bringing Mr. Eastham in for questioning."

"Oh, that's good." She was relieved to hear it.

The detective asked her a few more details about the contents of the padded envelope, which she answered as honestly as possible without mentioning the SIM card.

"The envelope contained twelve sheets of paper containing a lot of scientific jargon about the revolutionary robotic design that would enable spinal cord injury patients to walk again. To be honest, a lot of it was over my head."

Schneider consulted his notes. "And what about this code you and Callahan were able to decipher?"

"Miles did that," she said. "You'll have to ask him. I don't remember what the message said, exactly, although there was some mention about a missing link."

"Okay." He dropped his pen and smiled. "I think that's all I need for now. However, please don't leave the area without letting us know, as we'll likely need you to testify in court before the grand jury."

She nodded, although the very idea was extremely intimidating. "No problem, I'm not going anywhere."

"Great." He rose to his feet and opened the door for her. "Just wait here, I'm sure Lipski will be finished with Callahan shortly."

His "shortly" turned out to be a full twenty minutes, and by the time the door to the second interrogation room opened, she was beyond antsy.

"Finally," she said when she saw Michael. "What in the world took so long?"

"Let's get out of here," he said, his expression grim.

She sensed he was mad about something but waited until they were outside the police station to ask, "What happened?"

"Nothing." He let out a heavy breath as he opened the passenger-side door for her. "They don't like it much when civilians shoot people, that's all, even when those people are carrying guns and holding innocent people hostage."

She could see that being a private investigator probably didn't carry the same level of respect that a detective did and wondered why he'd chosen that profession in the first place.

Not that it was any of her business.

When Michael slid in behind the wheel, she placed a hand on his arm. "Try not to let them get to you. I was blunt about how you and Miles saved my life and Abby's, too. And I can't remember if I thanked you properly for that."

"Not necessary, but I appreciate you sticking up for me." He pulled into traffic, then glanced at her. "Do you want to stop at the hospital first to see Miles, before I take you to pick up Abby?"

She hesitated, then nodded. "Sure, that works."

"I'm going to drop you off, then run over to see

if my buddy has finished up with the SIM card. I'll be twenty to thirty minutes, tops."

"Sounds good." She twisted her fingers together, suddenly nervous about seeing Miles alone. During their intense time together, she'd always had Abby with her as a buffer.

Granted, being in the hospital wasn't exactly alone. There would be nurses and other hospital staff around.

She took several deep breaths, reminding herself that she and Miles were friends, nothing more. Okay, maybe she cared about him, maybe she'd even fallen in love with him, but so what? She doubted he felt the same way.

Paige hadn't imagined his reaction when she mentioned what a great father he'd be. He might like her, but not enough to take on a ready-made family.

Miles was the kind of guy who took his responsibility seriously. He'd promised to keep her safe, and he had. She could see him continuing to befriend her and Abby, but nothing more.

She licked her dry lips. Maybe she should do both of them a favor and say goodbye.

"You okay?" Michael asked, his expression mirroring his concern.

She pasted a smile on her face. "Yes, I'm fine." She belatedly realized he'd pulled up in front of the hospital's main entrance. "Okay, I'll see you in roughly thirty minutes?"

"Yep."

She pushed open the car door and stepped out, enjoying the mild temperature. Michael waved at her as he drove away, and she resolutely turned and walked inside the building.

Trinity Medical Center was an impressive facility, housing the only level one trauma center in the city of Milwaukee. She retraced her steps from last night, finding the proper set of elevators that would take her to the third floor.

The hallways were busy with hospital personnel, although Miles's room was down at the end of the corridor, near a stairwell. She walked over to the doorway, listening for a moment to make sure she wasn't interrupting any personal care.

The room was silent, so she knocked lightly on the door, hoping he wasn't sleeping. "Miles? It's me, Paige."

"Come in."

His voice sounded strained, and she thought he must be in a lot of pain. She pushed open the door and walked into the room. "Hey, are you okay? Do you want me to find your nurse?"

"Well, well, if it isn't Mrs. Paige Olson."

She froze when she saw the man standing on the opposite side of Miles's bed, her eyes widening in horror as she realized he was holding a gun.

"Leave her alone, Eastham," Miles rasped. "She's not a part of this."

Eastham? As in the owner of ACE Intel? The guy the police were supposedly bringing in for questioning?

"Oh, but I believe she is." His smile was feral and she instinctively took a step backward.

"Don't move," Eastham said in a harsh tone, as he rounded the bed, keeping the gun trained on her. "You have something that belongs to me. And I want it back."

Paige shot a helpless look at Miles. She didn't have the SIM card, Michael did.

Only Michael wasn't there because he'd dropped her off. Unfortunately, she and Miles were on their own.

SEVENTEEN

Miles debated pushing the call button to get help, but he was fairly certain that if a nurse came into the room, Eastham would only take her hostage, too. He'd prefer the cops, but he couldn't summon the authorities from his hospital bed without Eastham noticing.

Right now, they had the upper hand. Eastham wanted the SIM card and likely wouldn't hurt anyone until he had it.

A wave of fury hit hard when Eastham grabbed Paige's arm and shoved his gun into her side. Never in his life had he felt this powerless. Not even when Dawn was dying. "Let her go," he bit out.

"Where is it?" Eastham hissed. "Sasha told me that Whitfield solved the technology glitch and documented his findings. Where is the information now?"

"In a safe place," Paige said. Her voice was

steady, but her wide eyes behind her glasses betrayed the depth of her fear.

"Fine. That means we're going for a little ride." Eastham nudged her with the gun, making her wince.

"No. I'll go." Miles swung his legs over the edge of the bed, ignoring the shaft of pain that shot through his chest and down his arm. He grabbed on to the side rail of the bed with his uninjured arm to steady himself. "Whitfield sent the information to me. She's just an innocent bystander."

"You just had surgery. You can't leave the hospital," Paige protested.

"I can and I will." He was grateful to be wearing pajama pants beneath his hospital gown. The room spun for a moment, then righted itself.

"Miles, please stay," Paige begged, then glanced at Eastham. "I need to call Michael Callahan. He's the one who actually has the information, but I'm sure he'll meet us wherever you want him to."

"She's right," Miles agreed. "My brother has what you need. Here, I'll call him right now."

"No!" Eastham barked when Miles reached for the phone sitting on his bedside table. "No one calls but me."

Nodding in agreement, he dropped his hand. "I'll give you the number."

Keeping the gun up against Paige's side, Eastham lifted the handset, placed it on the table and punched in the numbers Miles recited.

There was ringing, but then the call went to Mike's voice mail. Regret roiled through him when he noticed Paige's shoulders slump. He hated the fact that she was in danger, yet again.

Eastham disconnected from the call. "Enough stalling. You're going to take me to where the information is. There's a stairwell right outside this room." He prodded Paige in the side. "Start walking."

The flash of helplessness in Paige's eyes sliced Miles's heart. He couldn't bear the thought of her leaving with Eastham at gunpoint. If only he'd told Michael to bring the SIM card here.

"I'm coming with you." Miles ripped the IV out of his arm and stuffed his feet into a pair of hospital slippers. "Trust me, my brother will bring what you want to save me."

Eastham hesitated, then nodded. "Fine. One wrong move and you're both dead."

It wasn't likely he'd kill them yet, but Miles wasn't about to argue with him, either. A wave of dizziness washed over him, forcing him to put his hand against the wall to steady himself. For a moment he closed his eyes and prayed for God to keep them safe. Especially Paige.

"You first, Callahan," Eastham said, keeping Paige close to his side. The owner of ACE Intel was smart; he knew Miles wouldn't do anything crazy with Paige's life at stake.

Miles drew the door open and stepped out in the hall. When he saw his brother standing there, he gaped and gestured with his hand toward the stairwell, silently telling him to hide.

Mike must have been listening at the door, because he instantly ducked into the stairwell. Miles felt calmer now, knowing they weren't completely alone, and took a few steps forward, glancing around to make sure no one was paying any attention.

There was a bit of commotion in a room near the nurse's station, some sort of medical emergency by the way people were scurrying around, so Miles glanced at Eastham and Paige. "We're clear."

"Into the stairwell," Eastham ordered.

Miles walked toward the door, trying to formulate a plan. He had to assume Eastham would push Paige through the doorway first, holding the gun on her from behind. Having the element of surprise would work to their advantage, and he could only hope and pray that Eastham wouldn't shoot Paige outright knowing that the sound of gunfire would bring people running.

Taking a steadying breath, he pushed open the door leading into the stairwell. From the corner of his eye he could see that Mike was flattened against the wall to the right of the doorway, but he made sure not to move his head or glance in that direction.

The landing wasn't large, so Miles had little choice but to take a step down onto the first stair. Then he turned and glanced back as Paige came through the doorway.

Mike waited until Eastham's gun was visible before making his move. Miles anticipated the moment of his brother's attack, grabbing Paige's arm and tugging her down and out of the way, while stepping back up on the landing so that he stood between her and Eastham.

Mike twisted the gun away from Eastham, and then turned the weapon on the other man. "Don't move."

The guy didn't listen. He abruptly turned and ran down the hall of the hospital, dodging between the hospital staff who were still working in the room near the nurse's station. Miles heard someone shout at Eastham to watch where he was going but the guy continued to run.

"Come on, we need to notify security," Miles urged. He glanced at Paige. "Are you all right?"

"I'm fine, you're the one who ripped out your

IV." She looked annoyed, but he was just grateful they'd managed to get away from Eastham.

"I notified the police before I came up here," Mike told him. "They should arrive any minute."

"How did you know to do that?" Paige asked. "I was afraid we'd have to stall for thirty minutes until you returned."

"I noticed the red Jeep parked in the parking lot," Mike said. "It looked like the one that followed me, so I had a friend run the license plate. It was registered to Krantz, aka Sasha Jorgensen. Since she's still locked up in jail, I knew that Eastham must be the one driving it."

"Look, here come the police and security now," Miles said with relief.

"I hope they have someone covering the Jeep," Mike muttered. "Or he's going to get away."

"Everyone all right?" The first sheriff's deputy to reach them asked.

"Yes, but Aaron Eastham took off."

"Don't worry, we have him in custody," the deputy assured them. "We caught up with him when he ran into a patient in a wheelchair. Glad to know there aren't any other nasty surprises up here."

"This is his weapon." Mike handed the gun to the deputy. "I was able to get it away from him just before he took off."

"You've arrested Eastham?" Paige echoed, hanging on to Miles's arm. "He can't hurt us anymore?"

"Yes, ma'am," the deputy assured her. "I'm assuming you'll be pressing charges for attempted kidnapping?"

"Yes," she answered without hesitation. "If it means keeping him in jail, I'll absolutely press charges."

"I will, too," Miles added. "Eastham admitted that he wanted the information from Sci-Tech. I'm betting you'll be able to link him through some sort of money trail to Krantz, aka Jorgensen. I know he's the one who hired her and the other gunmen who were chasing us."

The deputy took notes, and it was several minutes before they'd finished giving their statements.

"So, it's finally over," Paige said in low voice.

"Yeah. It's finally over." Miles hobbled back toward his room. He wanted nothing more than to pull her into his arms, but there was blood dripping down his arm from where the IV had been, and to be honest, he wasn't entirely sure she'd appreciate the gesture, considering she'd been placed in harm's way once again.

Because of him.

Then he frowned, realizing she was here, alone. "Wait a minute, where's Abby?"

"Mom's house," Mike answered. "If you guys are okay here for a while, I'm going to pick up the information my buddy took off the SIM card."

"Mom's?" Miles echoed in surprise. His heart thumped in his chest, thinking about how welcoming his family had been toward Paige. He liked it, a lot.

"Miles? Miles Callahan?" A familiar female voice made him wince. He turned to see a blonde nurse he'd briefly dated.

"Hi, Sandra," he said, with a definite lack of enthusiasm. "How are you?"

"Better than you. What happened?" She took a step toward him, as if to put her hand on his arm, and he instinctively backed away, sliding closer to Paige.

"Work-related injury, but I'm fine." He didn't like the way both Paige and his brother were looking curiously at Sandra.

Sandra's gaze narrowed a bit when she saw Paige. "Well, glad to see you're doing all right, since I never heard from you after our last date."

Miles had no idea how to respond to that, so he remained silent. When Mike smirked, he sent his brother a dark scowl.

"Watch out for this one," Sandra said to Paige. "He's a heartbreaker." Then she turned on her heel and walked away.

"Way to go, Miles," Mike said dryly.

"Knock it off," he said, wishing that Paige hadn't witnessed Sandra's snarky attitude. "I'm sorry, Paige. Trust me, that was a really long time ago."

"It's fine," Paige said matter-of-factly, but she didn't meet his gaze. "Listen, I think it's best if Michael takes me back to pick up Abby. I don't want to impose on your mom for longer than she's anticipating."

Miles swallowed hard, realizing how much he didn't want her to go. Not until they had a chance to talk. Maybe he had earned his reputation as a flirt, but it was never his intent to hurt anyone. It was only about having fun, keeping things light. Social. Paige was the only one who knew the truth about how he'd suffered after Dawn's death. His lighthearted approach to women had been a way to keep himself from getting hurt.

"Paige, will you please stay? Just for a little while? I'll call my mom. I'm sure she won't mind."

Paige hesitated, then gave a jerky nod. "Okay, I'll stay." The words were encouraging, but the solemn expression on her face wasn't.

Miles knew that he needed to figure out a way to convince her to give him a chance. To prove that he'd changed.

Because his future would be bleak and lonely without her.

* * *

Paige followed Miles into his room, then clasped her hands nervously in front of her. Last night Maddy had mentioned how Miles had been a bit of a flirt, so she shouldn't be surprised to see one of his old girlfriends. Yet she also knew that Miles had buried his feelings after Dawn's death, so she didn't think he was being intentionally hurtful.

He was a decent guy. One she was sure would someday find the perfect woman for him. Unfortunately, that woman wasn't her. She had her daughter to be concerned with, and Abby had to be her first priority.

Yet, now that it was time to say goodbye, she was finding it difficult to find a way to say the words.

"You should call the nurse so she can replace your IV," she said, once he settled on the edge of his bed.

"Later." He held out his hand and she stepped close enough to take it. He surprised her by pulling her close enough that he could rest his uninjured hand lightly on her waist. "I'm so sorry Eastham grabbed you like that. I hate knowing I placed you in danger."

"It's not your fault," she assured him.

He stared at her for a long moment. "Paige, I know that we were thrown together by chance, but I want you to know how much I care about you and Abby."

She blinked in confusion. "I care about you, too, Miles. You've saved our lives over and over again."

A smile tugged at the corner of his mouth. "You and Abby saved me, too, Paige. You showed me the way back to my faith."

"I'm glad to hear it." She drew in a deep breath, telling herself that keeping Miles as a friend was more important than any romantic feelings she secretly harbored. "I hope once you've recovered from your injury you'll come and visit. I'm sure Abby would love to see you."

He tipped his head to the side, regarding her thoughtfully. "Just Abby?"

"No, of course not. I'll be happy to see you, too. I hope we can always be friends." She did her best to smile, even though she felt like crying.

"Friends," Miles repeated with a frown. "I was hoping for more."

What? She must not have heard him correctly. "I don't understand."

"After losing Dawn to cancer, I avoided serious relationships. I lost a part of my faith and I didn't want to open myself up to that kind of pain, ever again. But that was before I met you." He tightened his grasp on her hand. "You've changed my life, Paige. You and your daughter. You're probably not going to believe me, but I've fallen in love with you. With both of you."

He's right, she thought. *I don't believe him.*

"Miles." She placed the palm of her hand against his cheek, the way her daughter had done last night. "There's no need to rush into anything. You've just had surgery, and right now you need to focus on recovering."

He mimicked her gesture, cupping her cheek with his much larger hand. "This isn't about being injured. I know how I feel and that's not going to change. My heart belongs to you and to Abby. I know it might be too soon for you, but I'm willing to wait. I'm just asking that you give me a chance. A chance to prove I've changed."

His response was unexpected. Travis would have tried to convince her that he was the best thing for her and that she couldn't live without him. Miles was putting her feelings first.

At that moment, she understood that walking away from Miles Callahan wasn't an option. And maybe, just maybe, being here with him was part of God's plan.

"Oh, Miles." She kissed his hand, then searched his gaze. "Of course I'll give you a chance. How can I not? I've fallen in love with you, too."

"Really?" The stark hope in his clear blue eyes made her smile.

"Yes. Really." She moved closer, gingerly putting her arms around his neck, being careful not to jostle his injured shoulder. "I love you, Miles. Very much."

He kissed her, then buried his face against her hair. "I love you, too, Paige. I'm honored you're willing to take a chance on me."

They held each other close until a knock at his door pulled them apart. She expected his nurse, but it was his mother who poked her head in the door.

"Miles? Are you all right?"

He grimaced. "Yes, Mom. Did you bring Abby?"

"Well, I didn't leave her home alone," she answered tartly. Mrs. Callahan pushed open the door and Abby skipped into the room, coming straight to Paige.

"Mommy! Miles!"

Thankfully, her daughter was still talking, although not nearly as loquaciously as she used to.

"Hi, sweetie." Paige scooped Abby into her arms, bringing her daughter up so she could see Miles.

"I hope I'm not interrupting," Mrs. Callahan said, glancing at Miles first, then Paige.

Paige hid a smile. "No, of course not. I hope Abby behaved herself."

"She's adorable. Of course she behaved herself." Mrs. Callahan's smile was sweet. "But I didn't rush over here just because I heard from Michael that you were in danger once again."

"Then why did you rush over?" Miles asked. The irked expression on his face made her giggle.

"Kari's in labor."

It took a moment for Paige to remember that Kari was Marc's wife.

"Isn't it a little early?" Miles asked with a frown.

"Three weeks early," Mrs. Callahan confirmed. "I'm sorry to drop Abby off with you, but I really want to head over to the labor and delivery unit. I hope you'll let me babysit again, soon, though."

"Tell Marc I'll be over to see my baby niece or nephew as soon as possible," Miles said.

"I will. See you both later." His mother left as quickly as she'd arrived.

"Did you have fun playing with the dollhouse, Abby?" Paige asked.

Her daughter nodded. "Lots of fun." Then the little girl rested her head on Paige's shoulder. "Missed you."

"I missed you, too."

"Me, three," Miles added in a husky voice. Paige noticed the softness in Miles's eyes as he looked at her daughter and knew deep down in her soul that the three of them were meant to be together.

As a family.

EPILOGUE

Eight weeks later...

On any other day, Miles wouldn't have minded lingering over brunch with his family, but not today. He glanced at his watch for the third time in ten minutes. Was it his imagination or was his mother dawdling over her meal on purpose?

When he couldn't take it any longer, he rose to his feet and began clearing the table. His mother had agreed to watch Abby for a few hours so he could have some alone time with Paige.

Not that he was complaining about being in love with a single mom. He adored Abby, but there were some occasions when three was a crowd.

He patted his pocket, reassuring himself that he still had the ring.

"I'll take care of doing dishes today," Maddy said, coming up to stand beside him. "I hear you're taking Paige down to the lakefront."

"Yeah." He didn't try to hide the goofy grin on his face. "We have the afternoon to ourselves." He gave her a one-armed hug. "Thanks, sis."

"Don't worry. I'll collect on some future date," Maddy drawled.

Paige entered the kitchen with a stack of dirty dishes. "Oh, I can do the dishes, Maddy."

"Not today," his sister said with a sly wink. "We're kicking you and Miles out of here for a while. Don't worry about Abby, she's enthralled with Kari and Marc's new son, Max."

Miles had been touched at Kari's decision to name her baby boy after their deceased father, Max Callahan. But he hoped they didn't continue the M name trend. After all, there were twenty-five other letters in the alphabet to choose from, and having all their names start with the same letter was annoying, not to mention confusing.

"Will you take a ride with me?" Miles asked Paige.

"Of course." She smiled up at him, linking her arm in his.

His doctor had given him the all clear to drive two weeks ago, but he still hadn't returned to full active duty. It wasn't the worst thing, since he'd been able to put together an ironclad case against Krantz and Eastham for conspiring to commit fraud and for the murders of Travis Olson and Jason Whitfield.

Not to mention, spending lots of quality time with Paige and Abby. He loved them more and more each day.

May sunshine filtered through the trees as he drove along the Lake Michigan shoreline. Paige was quiet, but the serene expression on her face portrayed contentment. Abby was back to her usual chatty self and seemed to accept that her father was with God. And his relationship with Paige had been going great.

Or so he hoped. Patting the ring in his pocket one last time, he turned into the marina parking lot and threw the gearshift into Park.

"Shall we take a walk?" he suggested.

"I'd love to." Paige climbed out of the passenger seat and gazed for a moment at the waves rippling in, splashing against the rocks. "It's so peaceful here."

He took her hand in his and led her down a winding path to a park bench that overlooked the water. Once she was seated, he pulled out the ring box and knelt beside her.

"Paige, I want you to know just how much you and Abby mean to me. You've brought faith, light and love back into my life." He took a deep breath. "Will you please marry me?"

She gasped when she realized this wasn't an ordinary date. He opened the ring box and showed her a beautiful square-cut emerald ring. He'd chosen the gemstone because he'd wanted something different from the diamond she'd once been given by her ex-husband.

"Oh, Miles, it's beautiful." She didn't reach for the ring, though, but looked up at him in surprise. "How did you know emeralds were my favorite?"

"You mentioned it once in passing, and personally I think the ring goes great with your green-gold eyes."

The fact that she hadn't answered his question made him wonder if she wasn't ready yet.

"I love you, Paige. And I want you, me and Abby to be a family, along with any other children God blesses us with."

"Yes, Miles." Her eyes shimmered with tears and she threw her arms around his neck, hugging him fiercely. "Yes, I'll marry you."

He closed his eyes in relief, hugging her close, knowing that this moment was the true beginning of the rest of his life.

And that this was all a part of God's plan.

* * * * *

If you enjoyed this story, pick up the first
CALLAHAN CONFIDENTIAL *book,*
SHIELDING HIS CHRISTMAS WITNESS
and these other stories from Laura Scott:

WRONGLY ACCUSED
DOWN TO THE WIRE
UNDER THE LAWMAN'S PROTECTION
FORGOTTEN MEMORIES
HOLIDAY ON THE RUN
MIRROR IMAGE

Available now from Love Inspired Suspense!

Find more great reads at
www.LoveInspired.com

Dear Reader,

The Only Witness is the second book in my Callahan Confidential series. I love writing series, and this particular one involving a large family has been especially fun. The Callahan family has a legacy of choosing careers that support and protect their community, but these jobs also put them in constant danger. This story revolves around homicide detective Miles Callahan, known as the fun-loving Callahan sibling. But deep down, Miles is suffering from the loss of his college sweetheart who died of cancer shortly after their graduation.

When Miles meets single mother Paige Olson and her adorable five-year-old daughter, Abby, he is determined to protect them. And it's not long before Miles realizes young Abby may be the only witness to a horrible murder.

I hope you enjoy Miles and Paige's story. I'm also hard at work on the next book in the Callahan Confidential series. I love hearing from my readers. If you're interested in contacting me or signing up for my newsletter, please visit my website at www.laurascottbooks.com. I'm also on

Facebook at Laura Scott Books, Author, and on Twitter @Laurascottbooks.

Yours in faith,
Laura Scott

LARGER-PRINT BOOKS!

**GET 2 FREE
LARGER-PRINT NOVELS
PLUS 2 FREE
MYSTERY GIFTS**

Love Inspired®

Larger-print novels are now available...

YES! Please send me 2 FREE LARGER-PRINT Love Inspired® novels and my 2 FREE mystery gifts (gifts are worth about $10). After receiving them, if I don't wish to receive any more books, I can return the shipping statement marked "cancel." If I don't cancel, I will receive 6 brand-new novels every month and be billed just $5.49 per book in the U.S. or $5.99 per book in Canada. That's a savings of at least 19% off the cover price. It's quite a bargain! Shipping and handling is just 50¢ per book in the U.S. and 75¢ per book in Canada.* I understand that accepting the 2 free books and gifts places me under no obligation to buy anything. I can always return a shipment and cancel at any time. Even if I never buy another book, the two free books and gifts are mine to keep forever.

122/322 IDN GH6D

Name   (PLEASE PRINT)

Address   Apt. #

City   State/Prov.   Zip/Postal Code

Signature (if under 18, a parent or guardian must sign)

Mail to the **Reader Service:**
IN U.S.A.: P.O. Box 1867, Buffalo, NY 14240-1867
IN CANADA: P.O. Box 609, Fort Erie, Ontario L2A 5X3

**Are you a current subscriber to Love Inspired® books
and want to receive the larger-print edition?
Call 1-800-873-8635 or visit www.ReaderService.com.**

* Terms and prices subject to change without notice. Prices do not include applicable taxes. Sales tax applicable in N.Y. Canadian residents will be charged applicable taxes. Offer not valid in Quebec. This offer is limited to one order per household. Not valid to current subscribers to Love Inspired Larger-Print books. All orders subject to credit approval. Credit or debit balances in a customer's account(s) may be offset by any other outstanding balance owed by or to the customer. Please allow 4 to 6 weeks for delivery. Offer available while quantities last.

Your Privacy—The Reader Service is committed to protecting your privacy. Our Privacy Policy is available online at www.ReaderService.com or upon request from the Reader Service.

We make a portion of our mailing list available to reputable third parties that offer products we believe may interest you. If you prefer that we not exchange your name with third parties, or if you wish to clarify or modify your communication preferences, please visit us at www.ReaderService.com/consumerschoice or write to us at Reader Service Preference Service, P.O. Box 9062, Buffalo, NY 14240-9062. Include your complete name and address.

LILP15

REQUEST YOUR FREE BOOKS!
2 FREE WHOLESOME ROMANCE NOVELS
IN LARGER PRINT
PLUS 2
FREE
MYSTERY GIFTS

✻✻✻✻✻✻✻✻✻✻✻✻✻✻✻✻✻✻✻✻✻✻✻✻

HEARTWARMING™

✻✻✻✻✻✻✻✻✻✻✻✻✻✻✻✻✻✻✻✻✻✻✻✻

Wholesome, tender romances

YES! Please send me 2 FREE Harlequin® Heartwarming Larger-Print novels and my 2 FREE mystery gifts (gifts worth about $10). After receiving them, if I don't wish to receive any more books, I can return the shipping statement marked "cancel." If I don't cancel, I will receive 4 brand-new larger-print novels every month and be billed just $5.24 per book in the U.S. or $5.99 per book in Canada. That's a savings of at least 19% off the cover price. It's quite a bargain! Shipping and handling is just 50¢ per book in the U.S. and 75¢ per book in Canada.* I understand that accepting the 2 free books and gifts places me under no obligation to buy anything. I can always return a shipment and cancel at any time. Even if I never buy another book, the two free books and gifts are mine to keep forever.

161/361 IDN GHX2

Name _____ (PLEASE PRINT)

Address _____ Apt. #

City _____ State/Prov. _____ Zip/Postal Code

Signature (if under 18, a parent or guardian must sign)

Mail to the **Reader Service:**
IN U.S.A.: P.O. Box 1867, Buffalo, NY 14240-1867
IN CANADA: P.O. Box 609, Fort Erie, Ontario L2A 5X3

* Terms and prices subject to change without notice. Prices do not include applicable taxes. Sales tax applicable in N.Y. Canadian residents will be charged applicable taxes. Offer not valid in Quebec. This offer is limited to one order per household. Not valid for current subscribers to Harlequin Heartwarming larger-print books. All orders subject to credit approval. Credit or debit balances in a customer's account(s) may be offset by any other outstanding balance owed by or to the customer. Please allow 4 to 6 weeks for delivery. Offer available while quantities last.

Your Privacy—The Reader Service is committed to protecting your privacy. Our Privacy Policy is available online at www.ReaderService.com or upon request from the Reader Service.

We make a portion of our mailing list available to reputable third parties that offer products we believe may interest you. If you prefer that we not exchange your name with third parties, or if you wish to clarify or modify your communication preferences, please visit us at www.ReaderService.com/consumerschoice or write to us at Reader Service Preference Service, P.O. Box 9062, Buffalo, NY 14240-9062. Include your complete name and address.

HW15

WESTERN WP PROMISES

YES! Please send me **The Western Promises Collection** in Larger Print. This collection begins with 3 FREE books and 2 FREE gifts (gifts valued at approx. $14.00 retail) in the first shipment, along with the other first 4 books from the collection! If I do not cancel, I will receive 8 monthly shipments until I have the entire 51-book Western Promises collection. I will receive 2 or 3 FREE books in each shipment and I will pay just $4.99 US/ $5.89 CDN for each of the other four books in each shipment, plus $2.99 for shipping and handling per shipment. *If I decide to keep the entire collection, I'll have paid for only 32 books, because 19 books are FREE! I understand that accepting the 3 free books and gifts places me under no obligation to buy anything. I can always return a shipment and cancel at any time. My free books and gifts are mine to keep no matter what I decide.

272 HCN 3070 472 HCN 3070

Name	(PLEASE PRINT)	

Address		Apt. #

City	State/Prov.	Zip/Postal Code

Signature (if under 18, a parent or guardian must sign)

Mail to the **Reader Service:**
IN U.S.A.: P.O. Box 1867, Buffalo, NY 14240-1867
IN CANADA: P.O. Box 609, Fort Erie, Ontario L2A 5X3

* Terms and prices subject to change without notice. Prices do not include applicable taxes. Sales tax applicable in N.Y. Canadian residents will be charged applicable taxes. This offer is limited to one order per household. All orders subject to approval. Credit or debit balances in a customer's account(s) may be offset by any other outstanding balance owed by or to the customer. Please allow 4 to 6 weeks for delivery. Offer available while quantities last. Offer not available to Quebec residents.

Your Privacy—The Reader Service is committed to protecting your privacy. Our Privacy Policy is available online at www.ReaderService.com or upon request from the Reader Service.

We make a portion of our mailing list available to reputable third parties that offer products we believe may interest you. If you prefer that we not exchange your name with third parties, or if you wish to clarify or modify your communication preferences, please visit us at www.ReaderService.com/consumerschoice or write to us at Reader Service Preference Service, P.O. Box 9062, Buffalo, NY 14240-9062. Include your complete name and address.

WPBPA16R